BAIT & STITCH

A Knitorious Murder Mystery

REAGAN DAVIS

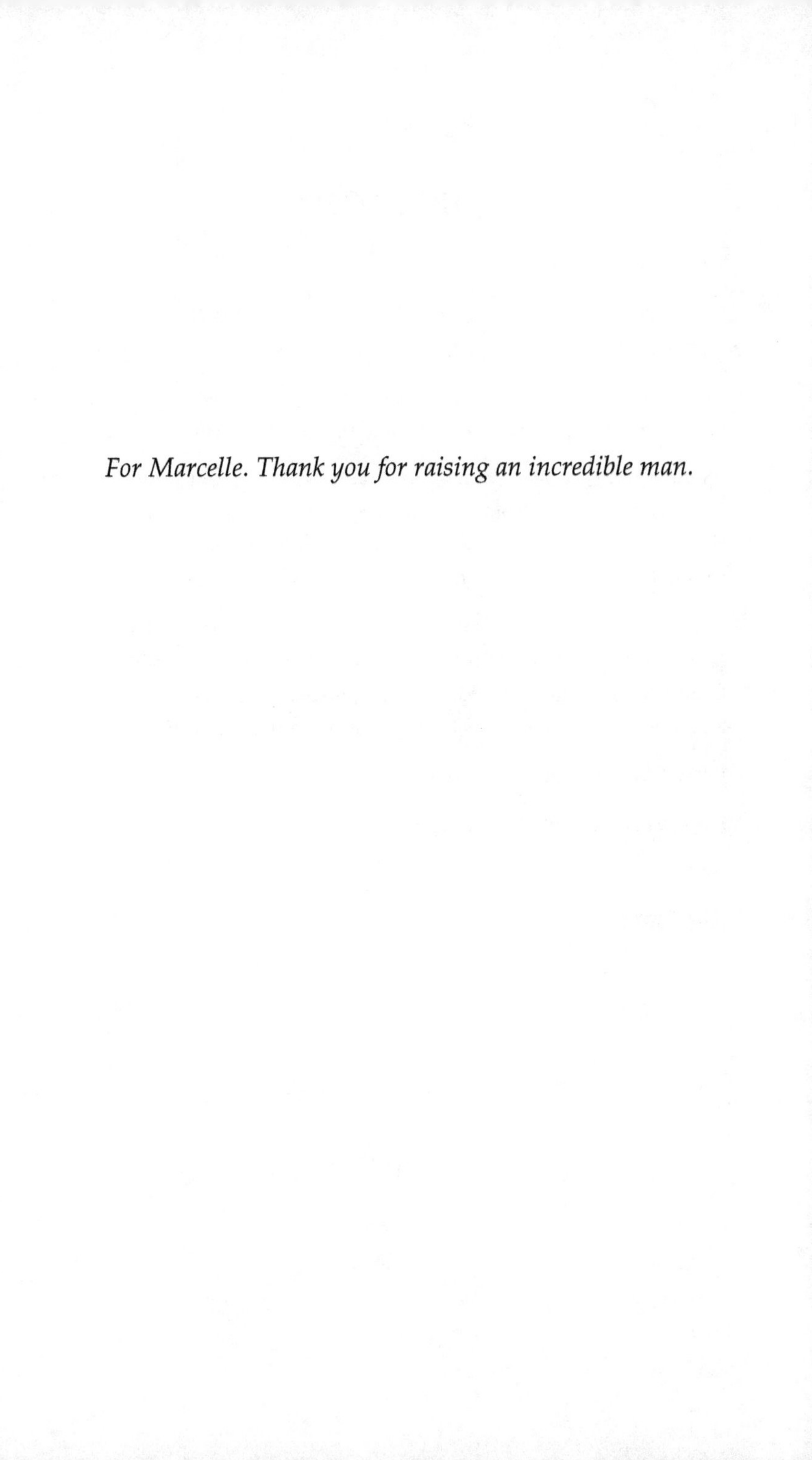

For Marcelle. Thank you for raising an incredible man.

COPYRIGHT

FOREWORD

Dear Reader,

Despite several layers of editing and proofreading, occasionally a typo or grammar mistake is so stubborn that it manages to thwart my editing efforts and camouflage itself amongst the words in the book.

If you encounter one of these obstinate typos or errors in this book, please let me know by contacting me at Hello@ReaganDavis.com.

Hopefully, together we can exterminate the annoying pests.

Thank you!

Reagan Davis

CONTENTS

CHAPTER 1

Friday, May 6th

I pop the trunk and unload the first suitcase, ignoring the warm, blustery wind as if refusing to acknowledge it, will stop it from blowing my hair in knots.

My hair is a tornado, and my face is the eye of the storm. Hannah points at my hair and covers her mouth, laughing at the Medusa-like curly chaos swirling around my head.

"Yours is just as bad," I say to my twenty-year-old daughter. "We have the same hair, remember?"

Hannah reaches up, still laughing, and tries in vain to tame her billowing brown curls.

I heave the last bag from the trunk and enjoy the satisfying crunch when it lands on the gravel parking lot. A fresh gust of warm wind rushes at me when I close the tailgate, blowing my wind-whipped hair swirls into a more frenzied vortex.

"Oh, goodness!" Connie giggles. "Look at your hair." She points just over our heads.

Mother Nature is kinder to Connie's sleek, chin-length bob. Her hair blows straight back, away from her face. The sun highlights every subtle tone, like individual strands of glittery silver thread.

"The view is beautiful." Hannah spins in a slow circle as she takes in the storybook surroundings, recording it on her phone. "I only have one bar," she complains, repositioning her phone farther, then closer to her body, trying to improve the 5G data connection.

"We're halfway up a mountain," I remind her. "Service might be spotty up here."

"It looks like a storm is brewing." Connie nods toward the heavy clouds in the distance.

"According to Eric's last text, a storm is heading this way. He's glad we outpaced it."

Despite wearing sunglasses, I shade my eyes with my hand and appraise the approaching grey mass. The distant clouds are like a predator, creeping closer until it can overtake the perfect spring day. I'm not cold, but a blast of warm wind sends a shiver up my spine, leaving me with an unsettled, ominous feeling.

"You've only been apart for three hours, and he's already worried about you?" Connie tugs the handle of her rolling suitcase, extending it to its full length. "I guess the honeymoon isn't over yet."

My face flushes at the mention of my new husband. I try to suppress a sheepish grin and act like the mature, forty-two-year-old woman I am instead of the infatu-ated teenager I feel like when I think of him.

The official honeymoon ended three months ago. But the novelty of being married is stronger than ever. I still smile when I sign my new name. Sometimes, I write my new name in my fanciest handwriting and just stare at it, savouring the rush of happiness that surges through me.

"What a lovely way to spend Mother's Day week-end," Connie comments, as we pull our rolling suitcases toward the main building. "Why didn't we think of this years ago?"

She isn't my biological mother, but Connie has been my surrogate mother and Hannah's grandmother for exactly half my life. I was barely older than Hannah when Connie and I met. Shortly after my ex-husband and I moved to Harmony Lake, my mum died. I was grief-stricken, exhausted, and overwhelmed. I was knit-ting during Hannah's naps and after her bedtime to cope and had knit through every bit of yarn I owned. One day, I rolled Hannah's stroller into Knitorious, Connie's yarn store, searching for yarn to replenish my stash. Connie took us under her wing and into her heart. We've been family ever since.

Connie is seventy years young. She is mostly retired. I own Knitorious now, and she works there part-time.

Inside the spa, we're greeted by a friendly employee who offers to take our bags and places them on a luggage cart. The lobby is warm and inviting, despite being large and somewhat institutional. Not institutional like a school or government building, institutional like a medical office or laboratory.

The floors are dark wood, but everything else is white, smooth, and uncluttered. Clusters of cozy seating areas dot the lobby, creating an illusion of privacy for the guests occupying them. Two large, black massage chairs line one wall, occupied by two relaxed, perhaps even sleeping, guests.

"Welcome to SoulSpring Spa and Retreat," says the cheerful lady behind the counter. "How may I help you?" The tip of her blonde ponytail drapes over her shoulder.

She is centred below the FRONT DESK sign. Technically, the front desk is not a desk. It is a long white counter with white computer monitors in the centre and at either end.

"Hi, Maria," I say, smiling and reading her name tag, *Maria C.* Underneath in smaller letters are the words, *GENERAL MANAGER.* "We have a reservation."

Maria cuts a quick glance at my hair. Twice. I can tell she's trying not to look but can't stop herself.

"Name?" Maria asks, tapping a keyboard somewhere under the counter.

"Sloane," I say. "Megan Sloane."

Maria continues typing but sneaks a quick peek at Hannah's hair.

Hannah must notice because now she's petting herself, smoothing her long hair from root to tip.

Maria doesn't give Connie's hair a second glance because Connie's hair looks like she stepped away from a photo shoot for an *haute couture* magazine. Hannah and I look like we're wearing tumbleweed hats made of human hair.

"Is the wind picking up?" Maria asks, her blue eyes twinkling behind the black frames of her large, square glasses.

"Sure is," I confirm.

"We're expecting some active weather later."

"I heard."

"Is cell service reliable at the spa?" Hannah asks. "I've only had one bar since we've been here."

"Our Wi-Fi is great," Maria says, pointing to the Wi-Fi password posted behind the counter. "The spa is between two cell phone towers. We aren't close enough to either for consistent service. Your connection might cut in and out. It's worse today because of the approaching storm." She shakes her head. "Electrical storms always mess with internet and cell service."

"Great," Hannah says, rolling her eyes and tossing her hand in the air as if she gives up.

"This is an opportunity for a social media detox," Maria suggests. "A chance to unplug and unwind." I sense she's given this speech before. "To tune into your inner voice instead of tuning into the constant barrage of the information age. Your mind, body, and soul will thank you for the break."

Hannah nods, her expression blank. She's not buying whatever brand of analogue inner-peace Maria is trying to sell her. Maria might be young—I'd guess early thirties—but she's not twenty and doesn't appreciate the place of prominence cell phones have in the life of a twenty-year-old.

Maria tells our room number to the employee who took our luggage. She nods and disappears toward the elevator. Another employee joins Maria behind the front desk. All employees wear the same spa uniform: beige cotton, straight-leg trousers with a blue, short-sleeved, collared golf shirt with the spa logo on the upper right chest, and a silver name tag on the upper left chest with their first name and last initial etched in black, uppercase letters.

"Enjoy your stay." Maria issues us keys to our two-bedroom suite.

Actual metal keys. Not card keys like most hotels nowadays. Each key is attached to a blue silicone, coil keychain that guests can wear on their wrists.

"Thank you," we say, almost in sync.

Our room is on the top floor. There are only three floors. We decide to be healthy and take the stairs instead of the elevator.

"There's no room number on my key," Hannah observes, flipping the thing over in her palm. "What if it gets mixed up with someone else's? How will I tell them apart?"

A sudden gale-force gust hurtles a tree branch at the window just as we walk past.

"Heavens!" Connie declares, flinching and clutching her chest as we instinctively cower.

Other guests rush over to investigate the crash.

"It's just a spring storm," Maria announces over the

chattering of the crowd gathered around the floor-to-ceiling window. "The weather service says the storm will be intense, but short."

Maria explains that intense weather is typical here and assures everyone that it will take more than a spring storm to topple the SoulSpring Spa and Retreat. Then she launches into the spa's history, explaining that it has stood on this land for almost one hundred years, weathering storms, floods, avalanches, and mud slides. We slip away from Maria's history lesson and into the stairwell.

CHAPTER 2

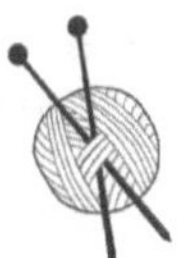

MY HAIR IS A LOST CAUSE. Thanks to the wind tunnel in the parking lot, my tight, defined curls are bushy, frizzy clumps. I give up, gather it in a top knot, and put it out of my mind.

Connie and I spend a few minutes knitting while Hannah walks around the suite, pointing her cell phone in every nook and cranny like she's scanning for trace amounts of something.

"What are you doing, my lovely?" Connie asks her.

"Recording the suite for social media." Hannah sighs. "Not that I have enough bars to post anything right now."

"The Shaws have arrived," Connie announces when someone knocks on the door that connects us to the adjoining suite.

April Shaw is my best friend. Her wife, Tamara, is a close second—next to Connie—and their daughter, Rachel, is Hannah's bestie.

After everyone gets settled, Rachel and Tamara head to the nail lounge for a Mum and Me Mother's Day Mani-Pedi, Connie and Hannah leave for the Free Your Mind Yoga and Guided Meditation class they booked, and April and I head to the acclaimed and award-winning spa restaurant, Epicurean Bistro.

Outside the bistro, we read Chef Nadira Patel's biography, which is posted inside a large frame just outside the door. Nadira is an award-winning chef specializing in vegan and Ayurvedic cuisine. As we read the long list of famous restaurants and spas where Nadira has worked as a celebrity chef, April nudges me.

"Listen," she whispers.

We hold our breath and focus on the silence.

"I don't hear anything," I whisper.

"Wait." She tucks a strand of long blonde hair behind her ear.

Then we hear it. Shouting. Then silence. More shouting. Still listening, we move closer to the source of the disturbance.

An irate guest is accusing Nadira of serving her chicken instead of tofu on purpose. The furious guest declares she is pescatarian and insists the chef sabotaged her meal. She uses words like "malicious intent" and "deliberate contamination."

"Why would someone deliberately serve chicken to a person who doesn't eat chicken?" April asks.

"Good question," I reply. "Nadira's grace and patience are impressive. I doubt I'd be as calm if someone was shouting, calling me horrible names, and tossing accusations at me."

The manager, Maria, appears and diffuses the situation. Whatever she says to the peeved piscivore has the desired effect. The outraged guest's voice quiets to a conversational tone. Heads turn away, and people return to whatever they were doing before the angry tirade distracted them.

April and I finish reading the chef's impressive biography, and highlights of her culinary career, then turn our attention to the posted menu.

"Oooh! Wanna split an order of Wagyu beef nachos?" I ask.

"Excuse me?" asks an unfamiliar voice.

A familiar woman leans close to me, giving me a good look at her face as she reads the Wagyu beef nachos description. It's the guest who just accused the chef of contaminating her tofu dish with chicken. And I just asked her to share a beef dish with me.

"Oh! I'm sorry," I declare, bringing my palm to my forehead. "My friend was right here. I thought you were her." I spin my head from side to side until I find April and point to her. She's perusing a menu posted on the other side of the doorway. "I-I wasn't suggesting you should eat meat," I stammer, hoping not to reignite the woman's anger.

My excuse is lame. April and the pescatarian guest bear no resemblance to each other. It would be impossible to confuse them. April is tall, and the woman is short, like me. April has long blonde hair, and the woman has shoulder-length dark hair.

"I recommend The Wagyu beef nachos. They're fantastic," the woman says, grinning. "I just ate." She shrugs her narrow shoulders. "But I'll share an order with you if you'd like."

I'm confused. Isn't this the same woman who just threatened to sue the chef for emotional pain and suffering for serving her meat? They have the same shoulder-length shag hairstyle, and the same piercing green eyes. They even have the same voice, though the woman next to me isn't yelling. I'm sure it's the same person. Did she undergo carnivorous conversion in the last five minutes? Whatever Maria said to calm her down was effective if it convinced her to become a meat eater.

"I thought you don't eat meat," I say, cautious of her potential reaction. "Didn't you just exchange words with the chef about a misunderstanding over chicken?"

April sidles up next to me, just as curious about the woman in front of us.

"I'm Summer," the woman says, thrusting her hand at me.

When she smiles, Summer's left upper lip curls more than the right, giving her a mischievous grin that makes me wonder if I said something funny without realizing.

"Megan," I say, shaking her hand. "It's nice to meet you, Summer."

"My twin sister, Autumn, is the angry pescatarian."

"I'm April, the hungry Presbyterian."

April and Autumn shake hands.

I nudge April's hip while stifling a laugh at her joke.

"This is Billie," Autumn says, gesturing to her ginger-haired friend.

"Don't feel bad," Billie says, shaking my hand. "I've known the twins since kindergarten, and sometimes I still mix them up for a minute or two." She chuckles. "We should ask Maria what her secret is."

"Secret?" I ask.

"Maria can always tell Autumn and Summer apart," Billie explains. "We got here on Wednesday, and she hasn't mixed them up once. It's incredible."

"Maybe spotting slight differences is Maria's super-power," I say, wondering what Maria noticed about the twins that helps her differentiate them.

If their best friend since kindergarten still confuses Autumn and Summer, how does a spa manager who just met them do it? Unless she's met them before. For all I know, they could be frequent guests.

"I assume you and Autumn are identical twins, and not the other kind?" April asks.

"Identical," Summer replies, "Right down to our voices."

"I'll say," I agree. "You even have similar hairstyles."

"Besides looking the same, my sister and I have similar taste," Summer explains, "which means our wardrobes are twice the size of everyone else's."

We laugh again. I like Summer. She's funny. And, at first glance, more laid back than her twin.

"It's easier to tell them apart when you know them," Billie interjects.

She and Summer recount a time when Billie couldn't tell them apart. It was Halloween. The twins dressed up as the twins from the movie The Shining.

"If we don't leave now, we'll be late for our appointment at the eyebrow bar," Autumn chides, checking her watch and interrupting Summer and Billie's Halloween story.

"Autumn, this is Megan." Summer gestures to me, and I offer my hand for Autumn to shake. "And April." She gestures to April, who extends her hand.

"Nice to meet you," Autumn says to both of us in a manner that is curt and efficient, but not rude. Then she gives us a small, tight-lipped smile.

"Likewise."

"Nice to meet you too."

April and I speak over each other.

"Let's go!" Autumn says, locking arms with her sister and Billie, dragging them away.

"Bye, Megan! Bye, April," Summer calls over her shoulder as she struggles to keep up with her sister.

"It was nice to meet you!" Billie adds with a smile as Autumn drags them around the corner.

My gaze lingers after the twins disappear around the corner. I know twins exist, and I've met identical twins before, but it still amazes me that there are people in the world who are physical clones of each other. I can't imagine looking into a face identical to mine or watching myself walk down the street.

———

Inside the Epicurean Bistro, the hostess seats us next to a window, and we flinch, making startled, gasping sounds when the wind whips an unsecured piece of nature toward us.

"The windows are reinforced glass," the server assures us as the wind rattles the floor-to-ceiling window. "But I can move you to an inside table if you'd be more comfortable."

We decide to trust her and stay at the table next to the window. Even with Mother Nature throwing a tantrum, the picturesque landscape is awe-inspiring, and I understand why there are so many floor-to-ceiling windows at the SoulSpring Spa and Retreat.

"Most of the twins I've met have the same features, but different senses of style. I can tell them apart by their hair or how they dress."

"Summer and Autumn appear identical at first glance, but there are some subtle differences," April says.

"Autumn is a pescatarian, and Summer isn't," I say.

"That's one difference," April agrees. "Summer was way more laid back than her twin. She was relaxed, chatty, and funny. Autumn was way more uptight. Everything about her is more tense than her sister. Even her smile was tense."

"Maybe that was because of the chicken incident," I suggest. "Maybe we just met her at a bad time." I shrug one shoulder. "Everyone has a bad day."

We're enjoying our order of Wagyu beef nachos and Springtime Palmitate salad when the light above our table gets brighter.

"That's better," April says. "Now I can see what I'm eating." She stabs a black olive and a chunk of Buffalo mozzarella with her fork.

"What time is it?" I ask. "It's too early for sunset."

April glances at her watch.

"We have a few hours before the sun goes down."

"Wow, it's so dark," I say, separating a chip from the dwindling pile of nachos. "I was so focused on the pleasant conversation and amazing food, I didn't notice how dark the sky had become."

"It's like nighttime," April agrees.

A crack of thunder booms in the distance.

"How is everything?" a soft voice asks.

We look away from the window. Chef Nadira Patel is standing next to our table. How long has she been there?

"Wonderful," I reply.

"This honey-lime vinaigrette is to die for," April gushes.

"I'm glad you're enjoying it." Nadira smiles. "It's good to know some guests are happy with the food."

"We heard your exchange with Autumn earlier," I confess. "You handled it well."

"The occasional dissatisfied guest is part of the job." Nadira shrugs. "It was an honest mistake, but it shouldn't have happened. The cooked, cubed tofu and cooked, cubed chicken were next to each other in identical bowls. I mixed them up. I should have stored them in unique containers and used better labels."

"You redeemed yourself with these nachos," April reassures her.

We laugh.

"Mother Nature is putting on quite a show for you." Nadira points at the large window, which is being pelted with loud, fat raindrops.

"We're hoping it will be one of her shorter productions," I joke.

"Without an encore," April adds, laughing at her own joke.

"I was here last spring too," Nadira says. "These spring storms are fast and furious. I'm sure it won't last long."

CHAPTER 3

"Hey, sweetie! Where's Connie?" I ask when Hannah joins me in the change room. "Isn't she having this treatment with us?"

"She said to tell you she's fine, but tired," Hannah replies, opening the locker next to mine. "She went up upstairs to knit and relax."

"OK," I reply. "I'm sure she'll find us if she needs anything."

"Aunt April, Aunt T, and Rachel are soaking in a hydrotherapy salt spa."

"Oooh, I like the sound of that. Did we book a session in the hydrotherapy salt spa?"

"Tomorrow." Hannah nods with a smile, reaching for the fluffy white spa robe in her locker.

"What treatment are we getting?" I ask as I fold my clothes and place them in the locker. "I know it has a clever name, but I can't remember."

"We're about to have a Soul to Sole Hydrating Body

Wrap," Hannah replies, gathering her long, thick curls in a messy bun and securing it with a scrunchie.

"Does it involve a massage? I could use a massage." I tighten the belt of my spa robe.

"First, they scrub away all the gross dead skin, then they massage us with hydrating lotions and potions from head to toe, then they wrap us up like burritos and leave us to marinate," she explains, tapping the screen of her phone.

"No phones in the change rooms, Hannah Banana!" I point to the large pictograph on the door—a cell phone with a red circle backslash.

"I'm turning it off," Hannah replies with a sigh. "I promised Lucas that I'd text him, but I can't get a good signal." She powers off her phone and sets it on top of her clothes in the locker. "The Wi-Fi isn't as good as Maria said. It's way slower than at home. It must be the storm."

Lucas is Hannah's boyfriend. She teases Eric and me, saying we are attached at the hip, but a wireless 5G connection attaches her and Lucas. Spotty cell phone service and slow Wi-Fi might give them withdrawal symptoms.

We close our lockers and pause mid-step, looking up at the ceiling when the lights dim, flicker back to full power, dim again, then return full power again.

"I hope we don't lose power," Hannah says.

We exchange skeptical sideways glances as we exit the change room.

———

SMOOTHER AND MORE HYDRATED than a pair of dolphins, Hannah and I return to the change room after our Soul to Sole Hydrating Body Wrap. We get dressed, accompanied by the booming soundtrack of thunder rumbling outside. Each crack of thunder is quicker and louder than the one before it.

"Twins!" Hannah says under her breath as we head toward the change room door.

"Hi, Summer. Hi, Autumn," I say with my eyes shooting back and forth between them, hoping the correct name lands on the correct twin.

They're wearing identical white, fluffy spa robes, and their identical transparent plastic cups with identical white straws contain identical green contents.

"Hi, Megan!"

I recognize Summer's mischievous grin with the extra lip curl.

"Hi again," Autumn says, almost smiling.

April is right! Their demeanours and smiles are different.

"This is my daughter, Hannah."

"You're twins!"

Hannah's green eyes are bright and wide. Clearly, she inherited my fascination with twins.

"Yes, we are," Autumn says with a slight nod.

"This is so good," Summer says after she sips her green drink. "Have you visited the juice bar yet?"

"Not yet," I reply.

"Mmm." Summer nods. "I recommend the Green Powerhouse smoothie."

Autumn frowns at the spot on her wrist where her watch should be. I get the sense that Autumn struggles to relax more than her less-uptight sister.

"What's in it?" Hannah asks.

"I don't know, but it's incredible," Summer replies, rolling her eyes with bliss and savouring a long sip. "I've had one every day since we checked in. I'll miss Green Powerhouse smoothies when we go home."

"Maybe the spa will give you the recipe," I suggest.

"Yeah, maybe," Summer says. "The ingredients are listed on the menu. I could ask how much of each ingredient to include."

"We should go," Autumn urges, then sips her smoothie. "They won't extend our time in the sauna if we're late." She sips again.

As we approach the door, an employee walks in and calls, "Excuse me!" to the twins.

As the door closes behind us, the employee offers someone a hot stone massage, explaining that another guest cancelled at the last minute and the twins were on the waiting list. The door shuts before I hear whether her offer was accepted.

In the hall, Hannah's phone dings inside her pocket.

"Service! I have service?" She whips out her phone and unlocks the screen. "It's Connie." Her posture and face droop. "She forgot to pack a toothbrush and wants us to get one at the front desk. She tried to call the front desk, but the landline in our room keeps disconnecting." Holding her phone at arm's length, Hannah paces, searching frantically for a reliable signal. "How did Connie's text get through? I have no bars."

"Technology works in mysterious ways," I tease, pulling my phone from my pocket. "I don't have service either."

Determined to find a signal, Hannah continues to pace, holding her phone above her head, then as far from her body as her arm will stretch, then down low. I wait patiently while she repeats this ritual, without success, three more times. Defeated, she drops the hand holding her phone to her side.

"I'm craving one of those green smoothies the twins had," she says. "Do you want one?"

"No thanks," I reply. "Go to the juice bar. I'll get Connie's toothbrush, and we'll meet up after."

SUNSET ISN'T for another hour, but between lightning flashes, the sky is dark as night. Sheets of rain hammer the glass and blur the view outside the floor-to-ceiling windows lining the hall to the lobby.

A tearful woman wearing a spa uniform presses her cell phone against her ear as she rushes past. I turn to check on her, but a wind gust rattles the window next to me, making me recoil. A twig breaks free from the cyclone of debris swirling outside the window and flies into the frame. I rush past the series of giant windows. As I approach the front desk, Autumn is walking away from it. Her purposeful gait and stiff posture give her away. She returns my smile with a brief nod, then veers toward the stairwell.

"Mrs. Sloane." Maria smiles from behind her large, square, black frames. "What can I do for you?"

"Please call me Megan," I say. "Would you have a spare toothbrush? And I'm told the phone in our room isn't working."

"The storm knocked out our internet and landline," Maria explains, producing a basket from under the counter. She rummages through it, knocking a few bandages, alcohol wipes, and pregnancy tests onto the counter. "It happens sometimes. I'm sure normal service will resume shortly."

She smiles, sweeps the spilled items into the basket, returns it to wherever it came from, and pulls out another. "I know we have toothbrushes somewhere."

"There's no cell service either," I add, watching Maria ransack a basket of tampons, travel-size deodorant, and motion sickness medication.

The lights in the reception area flicker when a clap of thunder shakes the windows. The simultaneous flash of lightning floods the lobby with a brief pulse of harsh brightness.

"Hmm," Maria hums, shoving the second basket back under the counter and pulling out her phone. "You're right. No cell service." She looks at me. "It's because of the storm." She pushes her phone into her back pocket. "The toothbrushes must be in the office. I'll be right back."

As Maria disappears through the door behind the front desk, leaving me alone with the thunder and lightning, I convince myself that if Maria is unconcerned about the weather and the phones, I shouldn't worry either.

Maria and I have different definitions of *right back*. She's been gone for at least ten minutes when the entrance door swings open with the help of the wind. A police officer, holding her hat against her head, wrestles the door shut, then leans against it and inhales a sharp breath.

"Whoo! Windy enough for ya?" she asks, removing her campaign hat and smoothing her dark hair toward her tight bun as she scans the empty reception area. "Where's Maria?"

"Searching for a toothbrush," I reply. "She should be back any second."

"Twyla Proudfoot," the officer says, extending her hand. "Nice to meet you."

Sergeant Twyla Proudfoot, according to her name badge, is a tall woman with shiny dark hair, dark brown eyes, and a friendly smile. Her uniform is soaking wet, and water drops roll off the brim of her hat.

"Megan Sloane," I say, shaking her hand. "It's nice to meet you too. What brings you to the spa in this weather?"

"Phones are down. We couldn't reach the spa to check on everyone, so dispatch sent me to check in person."

I nod, smiling.

"I still don't have cell service, Mum," Hannah announces, coming down the hall with her cell phone in one hand and a Green Powerhouse smoothie in the other.

"Me neither," I confirm, checking my phone again to be sure. I look at Officer Twyla. "This is my daughter, Hannah." Twyla and Hannah exchange greetings. "Sweetie, would you mind going upstairs to check on Connie? I'll meet you up there as soon as Maria comes back with a toothbrush."

"Sure."

Without looking up from her phone, Hannah sips her smoothie and walks away.

A thunder boom shakes my insides, and lightning strobes in and out, creating temporary, exaggerated shadows on the walls.

"I don't have cell service either," Twyla mutters, checking her phone. "There's a satellite phone in my patrol car that I can leave with Maria until the work crews restore service. I'll go get it."

"I'll tell Maria you'll be right back," I offer.

Twyla nods, dons her hat, and pauses, staring down the door before opening it and venturing into the storm. Through the window, I watch Twyla's khaki uniform cling to the front of her body and billow behind her like a parachute. She presses her hat onto her head with her face aimed at the ground as she struggles against the wind.

After the longest toothbrush search in history, Maria returns empty-handed and shaking her head.

"I know they're here somewhere," she insists. "I remember unpacking them. We should have an entire box of unopened toothbrushes." She rubs her chin. "Where did I put them?"

"What are you looking for?" asks an employee, stepping behind the counter.

"The complimentary toothbrushes," Maria replies. "We have at least two dozen somewhere."

The employee walks to the other end of the long counter and pulls out a basket.

"Any particular colour?" she asks me.

"Any colour is fine."

"Soft, medium, or firm bristles?"

"Surprise me."

She hands me a blue toothbrush with soft bristles.

"Thank you," I say, taking the toothbrush.

"Floss?" she asks, holding up a travel-size package of dental floss.

"No, thanks." I smile, then look at Maria. "Officer Twyla Proudfoot is here," I say. "She went back to her car to get a satellite phone."

An ear-splitting explosion of thunder vibrates through my body. The simultaneous streak of lightning is so bright that I squint.

CHAPTER 4

Silence. Darkness. Stillness.

No landline, no cell phone, and now, no electricity.

Who knew silence could be so loud?

The ringing in my ears replaces the incessant buzz of electricity that my brain has spent my lifetime training itself to tune out.

I swallow, but the ringing continues. I force myself to yawn, hoping if I pop them, my ears will stop ringing. They don't. Maybe they always ring, but I don't notice because the constant hum of electricity drowns it out.

The sudden silent darkness is unsettling.

My tinnitus is either fading, or I'm getting used to it. "Megawatt?"

April likes to call me clever nicknames that are puns of my actual name. Her current choice, Megawatt, is fitting.

"April?" I call. "Over here." I use the flashlight on

my cell phone as a beacon to guide her. "What are you doing here?"

"Hannah's smoothie gave me a craving. I was getting off the elevator and heard the loudest boom ever. Then, the power went out."

Maria picks up the landline. "Great!" she huffs, remembering that it's not working, then slams down the receiver.

"Landline is down," her colleague reminds her.

"Thanks." Maria's voice is thick with sarcasm.

A breeze blows the stray hairs against the back of my neck. I spin around and a disheveled Officer Twyla is carrying her campaign hat and using her body to force the door shut.

In the confusion, I forgot about Officer Twyla. What took her so long? How far away did she park?

Twyla leans against the latched door, catching her breath and assessing her misshapen uniform hat. Her bun is still intact, but drippy strands of displaced hair hang around her head and face. Stained by the rain, her khaki uniform is several shades darker than it should be, and water drips from her cuffs.

"Are you OK?" I ask.

Twyla nods. "It's bad out there," she says.

"Did you get the satellite phone?" I ask, not seeing anything phone-like in her hands or attached to her duty belt.

"It's gone," she says.

"Your satellite phone is gone?"

"My patrol car is gone."

"Someone stole your patrol car?"

"Who would steal a police car in the middle of nowhere during a raging storm?" April asks.

"Mother Nature," Twyla responds. "She took my car when she washed away the road."

April and I rush to the window overlooking the parking lot.

It's too dark to make out the parking lot. Seconds later, we let out audible sighs of relief when a flash of sheet lightning illuminates the gravel parking area. It's still intact, and our cars are still there. *Phew.*

"I parked on the opposite side," Twyla explains, jerking her thumb toward the opposite wall. "I only planned to be here for a few minutes." She shrugs. "A mudslide created a river that washed away my car."

"It also washed away the only road in and out of here." Maria sounds more inconvenienced than concerned.

Maria dispatches the employee who found the toothbrushes to hunt down the maintenance person and start the generators. The employee retrieves a flashlight and disappears through the door behind the front desk.

"We're equipped for this," Maria explains. "We've only had municipal service for a few years. Before that The SoulSpring was off-grid. Between two huge generators and solar panels with batteries to store solar power, we can function off-grid for several days."

"Good," Twyla interjects. "Because it will be days before anyone can come or go. The city won't even be able to dispatch crews until the storm passes."

"What if there's an emergency?" April asks. "What if someone needs medical help or something?"

"I'm a trained emergency medical technician and a law enforcement officer," Twyla assures us.

"And we have a well-equipped first aid station."

Hopefully, the well-equipped first aid station Maria refers to isn't the series of overflowing, disorganized baskets she pulled out from under the counter earlier. Some medical emergencies require more than bandages and pregnancy tests.

"Maria's right," Twyla adds. "The first aid station even has a defibrillator. We'll be fine."

A few minutes of anxious silence later, the generators hum to life and artificial light once again illuminates the lobby.

"You're soaking wet, Twy," Maria says, now that there's enough light to assess the situation. "Let's get you dried off."

Without checking the computer, a book, or anything, Maria produces a key, hands it to Twyla, and mumbles under her breath.

"Thank you." The officer takes the key. "I'll be right back."

Spa uniforms trickle into the lobby. Maria explains that because the spa's intercom relies on the internet, she can't make announcements, and guests can't contact the front desk from their rooms. Maria informs her staff that she wants to do a headcount. She assigns employees to specific floors and sections of the resort, instructing them to gather every guest and employee and bring them to the Epicurean Bistro.

With their instructions issued, employees leave the lobby in pairs, heading to their assigned posts. April and I leave with them to collect Connie, Hannah, Tamara, and Rachel and bring them to the bistro. Worried about the possibility of another power failure, we forego the elevator and use the stairs to get to our third-floor rooms.

CHAPTER 5

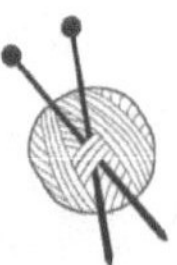

THE EPICUREAN BISTRO IS FULL. Extra chairs line the walls to accommodate everyone.

I'm knitting and listening as Maria reassures us that there is enough power, food, and supplies to run the spa for several days.

"What are you knitting?" Tamara whispers.

"Spa wash cloth," I whisper in reply.

"It's nice," Tamara says.

"Thanks," I say. "I'm making one for Eric's mum and each of my sisters-in-law. I'm going to purchase some artisanal soaps and stuff from the spa gift shop and make self-care gift packages for them."

"Good idea," Tamara whispers. "I wish I'd thought of that."

"I have more yarn and needles," I offer.

"Yeah?" she asks, her voice creeping above a whisper and causing a few nearby guests to give us *the look*. The disapproving, *please be quiet* look.

The worst of the storm has passed. The thunder is less frequent and more distant, and the wind hasn't wreaked any noticeable havoc since Maria approached the maître d' lectern to address us.

Craning my neck to look out a window, I glimpse Billie slinking in and taking a seat close to the door. We make eye contact. She smiles and gives me a small wave. I return the smile and wave with my knitting.

"And Officer Twyla is a trained medic in the unlikely event that anyone requires medical assistance," Maria announces.

Two guests, a registered nurse and a doctor, raise their hands and offer their professional expertise if necessary.

Officer Twyla must have borrowed clothes from someone because, instead of her wet uniform, she's wearing grey sweatpants, a white t-shirt, grey zip hoodie, and white sneakers. Her damp, dark hair is pulled into a high ponytail. It's much longer than the tight bun led me to believe.

"I'm sure we're all checking our phones regularly," Twyla says. "We're all eager for cell phone service to be restored so we can contact our loved ones. If anyone can make a call or send a text, please let me know right away." She smiles. "Thank you."

Maria takes over again, spinning a yarn about how this period of unintentional disconnection is *a wonderful opportunity for reflection and solitude,* and she hopes each of us *will take advantage of this mental space to embrace a digital detox* and *focus on introspection.* She's trying to reframe being stranded by a natural disaster as the universe providing us *a once-in-a-lifetime opportunity for growth and enlightenment.*

I would rather have cell service and a drivable road. Watching my digitally devoid daughter squirm in her seat and gnaw her lip as she makes yet another desperate attempt to find a signal by holding her phone up to the window, I'm guessing she'd rather have cell service, too, instead of *mental space to embrace a digital detox and focus on introspection.*

Instead of *reflection and solitude*, I'd rather contact my husband and let him know we're OK so he can relax and enjoy his weekend. And instead of *introspection*, I'd rather contact my ex-husband and assure him our daughter is fine, so he can stop pacing around his condo, trying to call her every thirty seconds.

Maria opens the floor to questions and hands pop into the air.

"Does anyone know we're stranded?" asks the guest. "I mean, if we can't contact anyone, how will they know we need help?"

"We don't need help," Maria reminds her. "We can function as normal for several days..." She repeats her spiel about generators, solar power, food, water, medical supplies... and ends with her speech about how this situation might be a blessing in disguise for those of us in need of a respite from the constant bombardment of online information.

Most people in this room have a loved one to worry about them. We live in the digital age, and people expect constant connection and instant—or almost instant—access to each other. By now, someone has figured out something is wrong at The SoulSpring Spa and Retreat. People know we're stranded, and they're trying to get to us. I know it. I feel it in my bones.

I have no doubt the local police force is wondering where Sergeant Twyla Proudfoot is and searching for the missing officer and patrol car.

Eric has texted me and is worried because I haven't responded. Lucas is worried because he hasn't heard from Hannah, and she hasn't posted on social media. He'll ask Eric if he's heard from Hannah or me. I'm sure Adam is panicking because he can't contact our daughter, and his panic will increase when he finds out Eric and Lucas can't contact us either. Connie's partner, Archie, will ask them if they've heard anything, and April and Tamara's teenage son, Zach, will contact them because he can't reach his mothers or sister. I'm certain that by now, they've figured out we're incommunicado, and something is wrong.

My husband is a police chief. He'll contact the local authorities and ask why no one at the SoulSpring Spa and Retreat is reachable.

Maria and Twyla answer questions and allay concerns. Then Maria takes attendance. Sensing that this impromptu gathering is almost over, I stuff my knitting inside my bag and sit up straight, ready to shout, "Here," when she calls my name.

Maria is more than halfway through the roll call for the second-floor guests when a flustered twin swoops into the bistro, rushing to the maître d' lectern where Maria is calling attendance. Squinting, the twin scans the room, searching the crowd.

"Autumn or Summer?" April whispers.

"Autumn," I reply. "Her posture is rigid, and her face is tense."

"Agreed." April nods. "She's wound up tighter than a two-dollar watch."

"Did you want to say something, Autumn?" Maria asks, miffed by the interruption.

Maria uses Autumn's name with confidence. Summer and Billie were right, she has no problem differentiating the identical twins.

"Where's my sister?!" Autumn demands. "Summer?" she continues surveying the room. "Has anyone seen my sister?"

The crowd murmurs and shuffles, searching their immediate vicinities for the missing twin and asking their neighbours if they've seen her.

"When did you last see her?" Twyla asks, now on her feet.

"In the change room," Autumn replies. "We were going to the sauna. My plans changed. I left and Summer went to the sauna without me. We had planned to meet in our room, but she never showed up." She looks at Twyla with pleading eyes. "I've looked everywhere. I've tried texting and phoning her, but I don't have a signal."

"No one has a signal," says a random guest. "Phones down."

"There's no internet either," adds another disembodied voice.

This information further increases Autumn's apparent distress.

"She has to be here somewhere!" Autumn's breaths are quick, and her chest heaves. She might be on the verge of hyperventilating.

Billie threads her way through the room and joins Autumn at the lectern.

"I assumed you and Summer were together," Billie says.

"I thought she was with you," Autumn retorts. "I haven't seen her since I left the change room. I had a headache and went upstairs to lie down."

Maria turns her attention to a group of employees seated to her right.

"Who cleared the sauna after the blackout?"

Two employees exchange timid smiles and raise their hands.

"The sauna was empty," says the first employee.

"The doors were locked, and the lights were off," confirms the second.

"We'll mount a search," Twyla declares.

She steps in front of Maria and addresses the employees directly. I can't hear Twyla's words, but they pay attention and occasionally nod in unison.

The murmur of the crowd grows louder with concern and speculation about the missing guest.

"Excuse me," Twyla commands with an authoritative tone we haven't heard from her before. The room hushes, and everyone directs their attention to the officer standing at the lectern. "In an orderly fashion, please return to your rooms and stay there. Since phones are down and you can't call the front desk, we will position an attendant at either end of each floor. Please speak to them if you need assistance. We'll knock when we've cleared the premises, and you can leave your rooms."

"Won't it be faster if everyone searches for Summer?" a guest shouts from somewhere behind me.

"No," Twyla replies. "Too many volunteers will impede the search. The best way to help is to stay in your room until we tell you otherwise."

"Will you be searching our rooms in case she's in the wrong room?" another guest asks.

"It's possible," the police officer replies. "We'll search common areas first. If you find Summer in your room, please notify me or an employee immediately."

Maria resumes taking attendance, and Twyla continues instructing the spa employees in a volume that's inaudible to the curious guests. She dismisses them, and they file out of the bistro in a single, paired-off line.

Maria completes the roll call, thanks us for our collective patience and cooperation, and apologizes for the inconvenience. We leave the bistro amid the muffled mumbles of people hoping for a quick and happy resolution to the search for Summer, swift resumption of cell phone service, and conjecture about where Summer could be.

CHAPTER 6

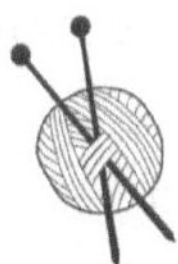

"Hannah mentioned she met the twins in the change room after your wrap session," Connie says as we inch our way toward the stairs. "She said it was the twins who encouraged her to try the juice bar."

"That's right," I say. "When Hannah and I left, they were talking to a spa employee about a hot stone massage."

"Do you think you should mention this to Officer Twyla, my dear?"

"Maybe," I reply with a shrug. "But not right now. Twyla's priority is locating Summer, and I don't want to slow down the search. Anyway, when they find Summer safe and sound, our encounter in the change room will be irrelevant."

"Mum!" Hannah weaves through the crowd until she's behind Connie and me. "Should we tell the police officer we saw Summer and Autumn in the change room?"

"I'll go with you," April jumps in.

"Fine," I relent. "If she can spare the time, I'll tell Twyla about our conversation with Autumn and Summer."

"I'll go upstairs with Connie," Hannah offers, taking her surrogate grandmother's arm.

I step out of line and loiter in an out-of-the-way spot while April tells her wife and daughter that she's accompanying me to speak to the police officer.

"Don't either of you go missing!" Tamara cautions as she files past with the crowd, wagging her index finger.

April steps out of line, and we slip around the corner, out of sight of the employee monitoring the stairwell entrance.

"Now what?" April asks, rubbing her hands together. "Are we going to talk to Twyla? Or should we look for Summer?"

"Both."

We decide it makes sense to start the search in the change room since it's Summer's last known location. We expect Twyla and Maria are already there.

The hall leading to the change room is dark, and we use the flashlights on our phones to guide us. April and I surmise Maria turned off as many lights as possible to conserve energy since we're relying on generators and stored solar power to run the place. On the way, I tell April about the conversation Hannah and I had with the twins.

"We left before I could hear whether Summer or Autumn accepted the employee's offer."

"Which twin did she offer it to?" April asks, opening the change room door.

"I don't know," I reply as we enter the dark change room. "The employee didn't address anyone by name. She was probably trying to avoid mixing them up."

April gropes one wall, and I grope another. I find a panel of switches and flip them. The lights flicker to life.

"They're used to it," April reasons, checking the changing stalls. "They're identical. I'm sure people have mixed them up all their lives."

"Maybe neither twin took the hot stone massage," I suggest. "I saw Autumn walking away from the front desk before the blackout."

I check the showers while April checks the toilet stalls.

"How could Autumn be at the front desk and on a massage table?"

"I don't know," I admit. "But I saw Autumn walking away from the front desk when I was getting a toothbrush for Connie. She was walking toward the stairwell. Then, Autumn rushed into the bistro searching for her sister. She told Twyla they were on their way to the sauna when her plans changed. She said Summer went to the sauna without her."

"You're sure the twin you saw leaving the front desk was Autumn?"

April pushes the door that leads to the hydrotherapy pools. It's locked.

"She had Autumn's intensity," I reason. "Her demeanour was uptight, and her smile seemed forced."

"Sounds like Autumn," April confirms. "If Summer was in the sauna, and you saw Autumn going toward their room, maybe neither twin went for a hot stone massage."

"Maybe," I concede. "When Autumn burst into the bistro searching for Summer, she said she was lying down in their room."

We scan the locker area. All the lockers except one are ajar. April approaches the closed locker and tugs the lock. It doesn't open.

"Summer and Autumn were standing near that locker when Hannah and I ran into them," I say.

"Do you think this could be Summer's locker?" April asks.

"I'm not sure," I reply. "But if it is, why didn't Summer return to her locker after the sauna?"

"It might not be Summer's locker." April dismisses my theory and drops the lock, letting it clang against the metal door. "It could belong to anyone," she reasons. "Guests probably leave stuff in lockers all the time, especially if they're coming back the next day for a treatment."

I point to the sign posted above the full-length mirror. PLEASE DO NOT LEAVE PERSONAL ITEMS IN LOCKERS OVERNIGHT. WE DISINFECT EACH LOCKER AND PROVIDE FRESH ROBES EACH EVENING. ABANDONED BELONGINGS WILL BE DISCARDED.

"Would Summer fit inside a locker?" I ask, standing sideways and sucking in my belly, wondering if I would fit inside a locker.

"That's morbid, Megnolia!" Horrified and amused, April gasps and smiles. "Summer isn't inside a locker."

The twins are taller but narrower than me. It wouldn't be an easy fit, especially with the hook and shelf configuration inside the lockers.

"She has to be somewhere," I reason. "If we don't find her anywhere else, someone will have to check the locker."

"Maybe Summer's stuff is in this locker," she concedes. "Maybe she never left the sauna."

We take cautious steps toward the door that leads to the sauna.

"You heard the employees in the bistro," I remind her. "Two of them told Maria the sauna was empty and locked."

"We should check anyway," April says.

I push the door that leads to the sauna. It opens. Success.

The lights are off, just like the employees said.

April feels along the wall next to the change-room door, and I fumble along the wall behind the reception desk. April finds the switch and lights up the room.

I lob my knitting bag onto the reception desk and take in my surroundings.

Across from the reception desk, four doors lead to four different saunas.

"That's a lot of saunas," I comment.

"According to this, each sauna is different and offers a unique experience and benefits," April says, studying a brochure she found on the reception desk. "The first sauna,"—she points to the first door—"is a traditional Finnish sauna. A low humidity sauna heated by a wood stove that heats stones to between 140 and 200 degrees Fahrenheit. Water poured over the stones creates steam."

I approach the first door and peer through the panel window.

"Empty," I say, then push and pull the door handle. "And locked."

I approach the second door.

"That's the infrared sauna," April informs me. "It's a high-tech option that heats the body instead of the room and creates no humidity."

"Empty," I confirm peering through the window. "And locked," I add, tugging the door handle. "What kind of sauna is this?" I ask, approaching the third door.

"Steam sauna," April replies. "Also known as a Turkish Sauna." She turns the page. "Boiling water releases steam into the sauna chamber. The temperature is about 110 degrees Fahrenheit. This type of sauna is especially beneficial for the respiratory system."

This panel window is higher than the others. I stand on my tippy toes to peek inside.

"Empty?" April asks.

I scan the room. The floors and walls are basic-white ceramic tile with matching ceramic benches built into the walls. In the middle of the room is a large pentagon bench covered in the same, plain-white ceramic tiles as the floors, walls, and benches. The pentagon centrepiece has an intricate mandala pattern on top made from ceramic tiles.

"What's that?" I whisper to myself.

Is there something on the floor? It's hard to tell if there is indeed something on the floor, or if the glare off the glossy tiles is playing tricks on me.

I squint and shade my eyes with my hand. The floor tiles to the left back of the pentagon differ from the rest of the plain white tiles. There's some sort of splatter pattern. I check the other side of the pentagon to see if the pattern is symmetrical. It isn't. The non-conforming design is green. I squint. Maybe it's not a design in the tile. Could it be a spill? A green spill?

I gasp.

"What is it, Megabot?"

"The twins had green smoothies! There's green on the floor."

"No food or drink permitted in the saunas." April points to the sign on the back of the sauna door.

I inspect the floor behind the pentagon again. A matte, white blotch interrupts the sheen of the polished floor tiles. Fluffy? A fluffy white blotch? Like a fluffy spa robe!

"It's her!" I shout, bouncing. "Summer is behind the pentagon."

I pull the handle, then ram my full body weight into the sauna door. Locked. I hurry to the reception desk.

While I ransack the drawers searching for keys, April rushes to sauna three and takes my spot at the window. She doesn't have to stand on her tippy toes to look through the glass panel.

"I think you're right!" she declares, her eyes darting around the room in a frantic search.

"C'mon! Where are the keys?!" I open the next drawer and groan with relief. "Found them!"

I grip one of the dozen-or-so keys and shove it in the lock. It doesn't fit. I grab the next key. It doesn't fit either.

April tears the fire extinguisher off the wall and runs toward the sauna door, her guttural growl increasing in volume and intensity with each stride.

I duck and leap out of the way as April releases a primal shriek and heaves the red metal extinguisher into the window. Shattered glass crashes to the sauna floor as she tosses the heavy extinguisher aside.

It lands with a clamorous thump, shaking the floor beneath us.

She reaches her long willowy arm through the broken window and unlocks the sauna door from the inside.

Thank goodness April is here. My short arm would not have reached the lock.

She carefully pulls her arm back through the opening.

I yank the door and run, lunging to the floor behind the pentagon.

There on the floor, wrapped in a fluffy white spa

robe, lies Summer. She's on her side. Her knees are bent toward her chest with her back pressed against the pentagon centrepiece. Her arm extends in front of her like she was grasping for something just out of reach. The other arm lays flat along her torso, her fingers resting on the curve of her bent hip.

Celery green splashes punctuated with intermittent dark green flecks create an abstract pattern on the floor. Summer's Green Powerhouse smoothie.

The cup isn't here, so I assume the smoothie originated from her intestines, as suggested by the strand of thick, green liquid stretching from the corner of her mouth to the floor and the stench of vomit lingering in the air.

"Is it her?" April asks from the door.

I look at her and nod.

"Is she?"

"Dead," I confirm.

CHAPTER 7

"WHAT'S GOING ON HERE?" Twyla demands, rushing through the sauna door. "What are you doing?"

I shove my phone in my pocket just as Twyla spots the body and freezes on the spot. I hope she didn't catch me taking sneaky photos of the scene.

"Deceased?" Twyla nudges her chin toward the twin's plush clad body and looks at me.

I nod.

Our heads spin toward the door when Maria gasps. Her hand clutches her mouth and, as if she just remembered something urgent, she turns and runs away.

"The defibri..." she says, her voice growing fainter as she disappears.

"Are you sure?" Twyla asks me, squatting next to the body.

I slide backward toward the wall, out of her way. She reaches two fingers under Summer's fluffy white collar to check for a pulse.

I shake my head. "We're too late," I mumble.

"You did this?" Twyla asks, pointing at the shards of broken glass on the floor.

"I did," April replies, tapping her chest. "I broke the window with the fire extinguisher. The door was locked. There were too many keys..."

Standing up, Twyla nods and raises her hand in a stop motion, cutting off April's explanation.

"You did the right thing," Twyla assures her. "You couldn't tell from the panel window if she was..." Her voice trails off at the end of her sentence, and she looks at me. "What else did you touch?"

I run off a list of things April and I touched, starting with the light switches in the change room. I'm at the part where I rummaged through the reception desk and touched everything inside, when Maria returns, out of breath. She thrusts a small red bag toward Twyla.

"Defibrillator," she explains, her voice breathless. "And I sent someone to track down the guests who identified themselves as a doctor and a nurse."

"Did you find her?" Autumn bursts in. "Summer?" she shouts, trying to get past Twyla, who's using her body to block the doorway to sauna three. "What's going on?!" Autumn demands. "Why did Maria get the defibrillator? Is it for Summer?"

Twyla takes a step forward, forcing Autumn to take a step back.

"Answer me!" Autumn demands, stomping her foot and pinching her eyebrows together as she glowers at Twyla.

Twyla opens her mouth to speak, but Maria offers Twyla the defibrillator bag again.

"Take it," Maria says, jerking her head toward sauna three. "Hurry."

Twyla takes the bag, and Maria rests her hands on her knees and rounds her back, still catching her breath.

"It's too late," Twyla says, holding up the bag. "She's dead."

"Dead?" Maria asks, unfurling her spine until she is upright.

"Dead?" Autumn echoes, trying to look past Twyla. "No. You're wrong. Let me check."

"I'm not wrong." Twyla takes Autumn by the upper arm and walks her backwards to one of the two chairs in front of the reception desk. "I'm sorry for your loss."

The backs of Autumn's legs bump into the chair. She drops into it and slumps forward, resting her elbows on her thighs and staring at the floor. She rocks back-forth in a self-soothing manner, dissociating from the surrounding scene.

"How?" Maria's blue eyes probe Twyla's brown eyes for an answer. "We've never had a guest die at the spa. Maybe she's just unconscious."

Maria takes a step toward the body. Twyla steps in her path. Guiding Maria by the shoulder, Twyla sets the red, zippered, neoprene bag next to my knitting bag, while gently lowering Maria into the other armchair in front of the reception desk.

"You sit here," Twyla says to April as she rolls the ergonomic office chair from behind the reception desk toward a far wall. Then she looks at me. "And you sit there."

She points to a leather armchair against the wall between the first and second saunas. Away from April. I've seen Eric do this. Twyla is separating us so we can't get our stories straight—or influence each other's recollection of events, as my husband likes to say—until she questions us separately.

I do as I'm told and sit in the chair.

"Breathe," Maria says to Autumn, placing a gentle hand on her knee. "In through your nose. One... two... three... four." Maria takes in an exaggerated breath to show her the technique.

Autumn averts her gaze from the floor and stares blankly at Maria for a moment. She ignores the spa manager's breathing advice, returning her focus to the floor, crying silent tears, and resuming her gentle, back-and-forth rocking.

"And out through your mouth. One... two... three... four." Maria says, exhaling louder than necessary as she counts.

Unlike Autumn, I breathe along with Maria and repeat my mantra, *heavy shoulders, long arms* in my head, trying to will the tension out of my neck and shoulders.

"I found the doctor," an employee says, holding the door for the guest who follows her inside. "But we can't find the nurse. She's not in her room."

"Where is she?" Maria asks. "We asked guests to stay in their assigned rooms."

"Lots of guests aren't in their rooms," the employee

explains. "They're visiting each other and gathering in the halls with wine and snacks." She shrugs. "One lady is teaching people to knit on the floor outside her room."

"Is it Connie?" I ask, certain I already know the answer.

"Yes," the employee replies. "How did you know?"

"Lucky guess."

"We can't physically confine them," the employee continues her conversation with Maria. "So, we've switched tactics, and we're trying to at least keep everyone on their assigned floors."

I try to tune out the conversation between Maria and her employee and focus instead on the murmur of hushed voices between Twyla and the doctor. Twyla and the doctor slipped into sauna three while I was distracted by Connie's impromptu knitting class.

Despite my best attempts, I'm unable to decipher specific words. I assume they are assessing Summer's deceased body. I wonder if the doctor can tell how Summer died.

Maria finishes issuing instructions to the employee who delivered the doctor.

The employee agrees to whatever Maria said and leaves.

"Excuse me," April calls to her. "Would you mind telling our families that we're OK but we're delayed?"

"Of course," the employee replies, smiling. "Third floor, right? The guest giving knitting lessons?"

"Right," April confirms. "Thank you." She smiles.

The employee leaves, and Maria turns back toward the rest of the room. We exchange weak smiles. She looks away, directing her attention to sauna three, like she's trying to figure out what Twyla and the doctor are doing in there.

Me too, Maria, me too.

After their discussion, the doctor joins the rest of us in the reception area. She pats her cream-coloured linen culottes and matching tunic until she finds what she's looking for. She slides her cell phone out of the kangaroo pocket in her tunic.

The only unoccupied chair is next to me, so the doctor claims it and sits, crossing her ankles and typing into her phone. We exchange smiles, and as much as I'm dying to ask her about Summer, I dare not speak for fear of being labelled nosy or uncooperative.

With a hand gesture, Twyla beckons Maria into the corner. She whispers something in Maria's ear, after which Maria takes the key ring from the reception desk and unlocks sauna one. Twyla enters and, moments later, beckons Maria to join her.

It's easier to eavesdrop on sauna one. My assigned chair is right outside the door. Trying not to be obvious, I shift in my seat and cock my ear toward the murmur of their voices.

"The walk-in fridge is full of food, Twy! You *cannot* be serious!" Maria hisses.

"Shhhh," Twyla responds. "It's just an idea, Mare! We need to preserve the evidence but leave the scene as untouched as possible."

Evidence? Does Twyla think Summer's death was murder? Who would murder her? Why would they murder her?

I look at April, who's already looking at me. She opens her mouth, then taps on her lower jaw to close it. Picking up on her clue, I snap my jaw shut. I didn't realize it was agape.

"Excuse me?"

Autumn's weak voice takes us off guard. This is the first time she's spoken since Twyla sat her in the chair. She's looking at the doctor.

The doctor smiles at her.

"How did my sister die?"

"I don't know," the doctor replies. "The coroner will perform an autopsy to determine the cause of death."

"She was healthy," Autumn pleads. "She's had nothing worse than a cold. Was it an accident?"

"I don't know," the doctor replies. "I wish I could tell you more, but I can't. Sometimes people die suddenly. It's rare, but it can happen. I'm sorry for your loss."

Tears stream down Autumn's face, and her chin quivers. The doctor rises from her chair and hands Autumn a box of tissues from the reception desk. Autumn nods in acknowledgment, plucking a tissue from the box and sobbing silent tears.

Maria and Twyla emerge from sauna one. Maria retrieves two notebooks and two pens from the reception desk. She sets them on top of the desk, then leaves the sauna area through the change room. Twyla hands

April and me a notebook and pen. She instructs us to write statements of everything that happened from the moment we left the bistro until she showed up.

"Got it," I say.

"No problem," April says.

"Eyes on your own papers," Twyla warns, pointing at us. "And no talking. No checking facts with each other. No reading each other's statements."

We nod.

Twyla and the doctor return to sauna three. April leans forward, trying to see what they're doing. According to the charades April uses to communicate with me, Twyla and the doctor are taking pictures of Summer's death scene with their cell phones.

Maria returns carrying a box of freezer bags, two rolls of decorative packing tape with a pink herring-bone design, a box of tented place cards, and a box of felt-tipped markers. She spills the items onto the reception desk. Twyla comes out of sauna three to collect the odd assortment, then returns to the scene.

I'm re-reading my statement, and questioning my use of excessive commas, when Twyla and the doctor emerge from sauna three. The doctor leaves through the change room, and Twyla uses the keys to unlock sauna four.

"April."

My face jerks up from my notebook at the sound of April's name.

"Yes?" April says.

"Would you mind answering a few questions?"

Twyla nods at the notebook on April's lap. "Bring your statement."

April rises from her seat and follows Twyla into sauna four. The police officer closes the door behind them.

After what feels like an eternity, the door to sauna four opens, and April emerges, followed by Twyla.

I scan April's facial expression for any hint about what happened in there, and whether she's OK. She takes her seat in the ergonomic office chair and gives me a reassuring smile.

"Ready, Megan?" Twyla asks.

I nod, standing up.

CHAPTER 8

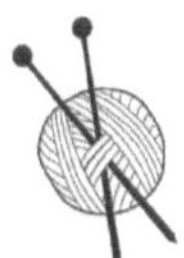

ON MY WAY to sauna four, I sneak a peek at sauna three. Twyla used the tented place cards as improvised evidence markers. She numbered each one and positioned it next to a shard of glass, or smoothie stain. She used the pink herringbone packing tape as crime scene tape, taping off the doorway in such a way that it would be impossible to enter or leave the room without disturbing it.

Inside sauna four, I hand Twyla my notebook. We sit on the cedar bleachers, and I wait while Twyla reads my two-page statement.

"Your statement is remarkably similar to April's," she comments.

Is Twyla suggesting April and I colluded to get our stories straight?

"Because we're telling the truth," I say.

"Why didn't you return to your room like Maria instructed?"

I explain how Connie and Hannah pressured me to tell her we saw Autumn and Summer in the change room shortly before the blackout.

"April offered to stay with me because,"—I shrug one shoulder—"that's what we do. We stay together."

"Why did you come here?" She points toward the floor, but I know she means here, the sauna area, not here, the SoulSpring Spa.

"April and I figured you would start searching at Summer's last known location. Autumn said she left the change room, and Summer continued to the sauna alone."

"Why did you break the window? Why didn't you report your suspicion to an employee?"

"Who?" I ask, gesturing around me. "April and I were alone. We would have had to go through the change room, and down the hall to find help. What if Summer was alive? What if she needed help? We didn't *want* to break the window. The first two keys didn't work..."

"I understand," Twyla says, interrupting my explanation. "But you must admit, it's weird that you found her so quickly. And by yourselves." She chuckles. "I mean, it's almost like you knew where Summer was."

"We didn't," I insist. "I told you, we assumed you would start searching here. We expected to find *you* here, not Summer. I'd never been in the sauna area before. We only checked in this afternoon."

"Did you touch Summer's body?"

"Yes." I nod. "I checked her wrist for a pulse. It's in my statement. I touched nothing else, I know better."

"What do you mean, you know better?"

"My husband is a murder investigator," I explain. "Actually, we met at a murder scene. I found a neighbour..."

"So, this isn't the first dead body you've found?"

Twyla's eyebrows disappear into her bangs and her pen dangles between her fingers.

"Not exactly," I admit with apprehension.

"How many dead bodies have you found?"

"By myself?" I ask, looking for a loophole. "One."

"And not by yourself?"

Uh oh. How do I explain this without coming across as a murder-scene groupie or serial killer? I look at the ceiling and take a mental inventory, counting bodies on my fingers.

My ex-husband's voice is in my head, telling me to refuse to answer more questions without an attorney. I would usually ignore Adam's voice, but he's a lawyer and his voice might be right. Twyla doesn't know April and me. She only knows that a few hours after we checked in, someone died under mysterious circum-stances, and we found the body.

"More than one," I admit, refusing to be more specific for fear of incriminating myself.

"Have the police ever investigated you as a murder suspect?"

"You think Summer was murdered?"

"I asked first."

"Look, I've found multiple murder victims. But in every case, the police arrested someone other than me. In every case, the suspect they arrested was convicted."

I'm struck by the bizarreness of this conversation as the words pass my lips. Twyla must think I'm a pathological liar, or a serial killer who has mastered framing other people for my crimes.

"Your turn," I remind her. "Do you think Summer was murdered?"

"I can't rule it out," she admits, "until the coroner determines the cause of death..."

"You have to treat it like a crime scene and investigate accordingly," I interrupt, finishing her sentence.

"You've heard that one before?"

"I have," I admit, with a nod. "It's one of my husband's favourite lines."

"What do you think happened to Summer?" Twyla asks.

"At first, I thought it was a tragic accident. Like maybe she slipped on the slick ceramic floor and hit her head."

"But you don't think that anymore?"

"If Summer had hit her head, it would have been obvious at first glance. Instead of noticing green smoothie on the white floor, I would've noticed blood. Lots of it. And her body wasn't positioned naturally," I reason. "It was too tidy, like someone staged it."

"Almost like someone tucked her out of sight," Twyla suggests.

"Exactly," I say. "Then I thought Summer could have

died because of an underlying health issue. Maybe she had a condition that was exasperated by the sauna. But Autumn told the doctor that Summer was healthy. She said Summer never suffered from anything worse than a cold." I take a deep breath and collect my thoughts. "Earlier, Summer was drinking a smoothie from the juice bar, but if she had died from an allergic reaction, wouldn't she have swelling? Or hives?"

"Not necessarily," Twyla replies. "The doctor says there are often obvious signs of anaphylaxis, but not always."

Twyla asks more questions, and I try to answer them in a way that doesn't make me sound like a person of interest or a true-crime fanatic.

When she finishes interrogating me, Twyla and I return to the reception area with April, Autumn, and Maria. In our absence, someone brought water bottles branded with labels bearing the spa logo. They're lined up on the reception desk, and April and Autumn each have a bottle. Either a thoughtful employee delivered them, or Maria fetched them while Twyla questioned me.

I join April, leaning against the wall next to her ergonomic office chair. Now that Twyla has questioned us, we can interact again.

"I want to see Summer." Autumn rises to her feet and gives Twyla a commanding stare. "Shouldn't I identify her? I'm her next of kin. How can you even be sure it's her if I don't identify her?"

Is she in denial? Or is Autumn desperate to see and touch her sister one last time?

"It's her," Twyla says. "Trust me. There's no trauma or damage that would make her difficult to identify. The doctor recognized her too. I'm sorry, but I can't let you see her."

"I recognized her too," I add. "I'm sorry."

"How did she die?" Autumn asks. "You must have an idea." She tosses her hands in frustration. "I need to see my sister," she pleads, her eyes welling up with fresh tears.

"It's not possible," Twyla reiterates, shaking her head. She positions herself so her body blocks the view inside sauna three. "Why don't you wait for me in sauna one, Autumn. I'll be there in a minute, and we can discuss this further."

Autumn opens her mouth as if to protest, but closes it again, and lets out a sigh of utter defeat.

"Fine," she mumbles, then shuffles toward sauna one, not even looking up when she passes the room where her twin sister's dead body lies.

Twyla closes the door behind her and turns her attention to Maria, April, and me.

"You can leave," she says to April and me. She opens a bottle of water and takes a long swig. "But please don't discuss this with any other guests or staff." She takes another sip and recaps the bottle, then picks up the roll of pink herringbone packing tape. "In fact, if anyone seems *too* interested in what you saw or obsessed with Summer's death, let me know immediately."

"Twy, won't *everyone* be interested in what happened?" Maria asks. "The staff are already discussing it amongst themselves, and I'm sure the guests are too."

"It's human nature," April adds. "People need to make sense of death. They look to one another for answers and reassurance."

"That's normal," Twyla says, tearing a strip of tape with her teeth and stretching it across the space where the glass window panel used to be. "If someone seems more interested than everyone else, or won't talk about anything else, I need to know."

She tears another piece of tape with her teeth. "You'll know if someone is too interested. Their interest will be noticeable and might make you uncomfortable."

April and I share a glance that says *we better be careful*.

My husband likes to say I'm made of questions. He worries that one day, I'll ask the wrong question to the wrong person and get myself in trouble.

"What am I supposed to say when guests and staff ask questions?" Maria asks. "I can't deny that someone died in the sauna."

"Admit that someone died. Admit it was Summer—after I talk to Autumn and get her agreement to disclose Summer's identity. But say nothing that will fuel speculation."

"Speculation about what?"

"How she died." Twyla stretches another piece of tape across the window. "We wouldn't want anyone to think Summer was murdered."

"Murdered?" Maria demands.

"I can't say for certain yet. But we should disclose as little information as possible."

"So the guests and staff don't panic?" Maria asks.

"So the murderer doesn't panic," Twyla clarifies.

CHAPTER 9

"Twyla thinks someone murdered Summer!" April declares as we leave the saunas and make our way through the change room. "Did you see her face when she asked us not to speculate about Summer's death?"

"Yes," I nod. "It's the same look Eric has when he's waiting for the coroner to declare someone's death was murder. He knows in his gut it was murder, but he won't say it out loud until it's official."

"Exactly," April says, pulling open the change room door.

We step into the dark hall and pause while we remind ourselves which way to go.

"This way," I say, turning left. "How's your arm? And your hand?"

"Fine," she replies, wiggling her fingers. "Why?"

"I thought you might have hurt yourself when you Hulk-smashed the fire extinguisher through the window."

"I'm fine," she says, examining her hands in the dark. "Anyway, if I pulled something, I'll book a hand massage with a massage therapist tomorrow."

"If they clear the road tomorrow, do you want to leave?" I ask.

April opens her mouth to answer, but confusion clouds her face.

"Didn't you have your knitting bag when we went in there?" she asks, jerking her head behind us.

"Mothballs!" I mutter. "I left it on the reception desk."

We retrace our steps through the change room.

"Sorry!" I say to Maria and Twyla.

Pink herringbone packing tape covers the panel window in the door to sauna three. The door is closed, and more pink herringbone tape seals the crack where the door and the doorframe meet. Twyla stands guard as Maria goes through the keys on the key ring, one at a time, trying to lock the door.

"You forgot something." Twyla nods at my knitting bag on the desk, next to the defibrillator bag.

"My knitting," I explain.

"I know." She grins. "I searched it."

I pick up the bag.

"Sorry for the interruption," April says, pulling open the change room door.

"Summer?" Billie shouts, charging through the open door. She scans the room, her eyes darting from person to person, before landing on Twyla. "Is it true you found Summer?" Her eyes are wide and intense, and I think she's holding her breath.

Maria stops fidgeting with the key ring and looks from Billie to Twyla.

"Where did you hear that?" Twyla asks.

"The employees on our floor said so. To each other, not to me. I was eavesdropping. They said Summer is in the sauna. Autumn?" Billie stares at Autumn, who is now standing in the doorway to sauna one, her gaze fixed on the floor. "What's happening?"

Autumn remains silent. Billie inches toward her, trying without success to make eye contact. "Autumn?"

Autumn gives no indication that she hears Billie's voice.

"The employees said something is wrong with Summer," Billie says, directing her words at Twyla. "They said Maria got the defibrillator." Her eyes dart between us so fast it's like she's trying to make eye contact with all of us at once. "What happened?"

"She's dead," Autumn says, her voice thick with emotion. She looks up at Billie with red, swollen eyes. "My sister is dead."

"What?" Billie's eyes grow wider and glassier. "No." She furrows her brows together and sucks in a sharp breath. "Dead?"

"I'm sorry for your loss," Twyla interjects, confirming the truth without saying it.

Billie slaps her hand to her mouth, her panicked eyes searching the room. Just as her upper body heaves, her eyes narrow on something under the reception desk. She lurches, grabs the trash can, grips it like a steering wheel, and holds it near her face as she throws up. Billie's body shakes, and she retches loudly as the green, smoothie-coated contents of her stomach spew into the basket.

———

"Are you OK?" April asks me as we climb the first flight of stairs toward our rooms.

"I'm fine," I reply, clutching my small knitting bag tight against my stomach. "Billie's reaction took me by surprise. I don't think I'll ever have another smoothie again."

"Some people have weak stomachs," April surmises. "They have a physical reaction to upsetting news."

I know April is right, but I can't shake the feeling there's more to Billie's reaction than meets the eye. She escalated from shock to disbelief to physical purging in a matter of seconds. Who processes information that fast? Eric says there is no such thing as a normal reaction to shocking news. But there must be a spectrum of normal reactions, right? I wonder where Billie's reaction would be on the shock spectrum.

———

April and I enter our respective rooms and use the adjoining door between the suites to gather everyone in one room. Together, we detail to our modern family everything that happened after Maria's update.

"My goodness!" Connie gasps. "That poor girl!" She shakes her head and makes a clicking sound with her tongue. "She was so young. Summer had her entire life ahead of her. Such a tragedy."

"Did Twyla say Summer was, without a doubt, murdered?" Tamara asks, wrapping her kinky hair in the silk hair-wrap she wears to bed. "Or is she speculating? People don't get murdered at the spa on Mother's Day weekend!"

"She seemed pretty convinced that Summer's death wasn't an accident or underlying medical issue," April replies.

"I hope someone is fixing the cell towers or whatever the storm knocked out. We need to call for help," Hannah interjects.

"Speaking of cell phones," Rachel adds, "on our way upstairs, we stopped at the kitchen and asked for some aluminum foil."

"We made antennae," Hannah adds, holding up a long rolled-up piece of aluminum foil.

More configurations of aluminum foil antennae are piled on the writing desk.

"For what?" April asks.

"For cell phone reception," Rachel replies. "If we don't have cell service by morning, Hannah and I will hike up the mountain and use the antennae to find a signal."

"And we'll call for help," Hannah concludes.

"Is that a good idea?" I ask. "What if you get lost? How will we call for help to find you? What if you get hurt? What if the ground is muddy from the storm and you slide away?"

"Relax, Mum," Hannah says, rolling her eyes so far back in her head her irises disappear. "We're not kids. We'll be careful, and we won't go far. I am capable of good judgment, you know."

I take a deep breath and remind myself that Hannah is my adult daughter, not a child. I don't have veto power anymore.

"Sweetie, I know you'll be careful, but I still worry. I can't help it. I'm proud of you and Rachel for coming up with a plan, and I know you'll be careful."

"But in the interest of safety," Connie interjects, "I think it would be best to stick together until Twyla solves this mystery or we can return to civilization, whichever comes first."

"Connie is right," Tamara agrees. "There's safety in numbers. Let's agree we won't go anywhere alone."

We nod and mumble our agreement.

"And let's keep our eyes and ears open for anything that might be related to Summer's death," I add.

"Of course."

"Obviously."

"For sure."

"Absolutely."

"You don't have to ask me twice."

CHAPTER 10

The Epicurean Bistro's dining room is almost empty.

Connie and I linger over a second cup of coffee, sitting on opposite sides of a table that's far too big for two people.

"Looks like it's just us, my dear," Connie says, then sips her coffee.

"Here's to quality time," I respond, then take a long sip of hazelnut-maple latte.

April and Tamara have already left for a morning of reiki treatments and acupuncture. Hannah and Rachel barely finished their bagels and yogurt parfaits before rushing upstairs to collect their homemade antennae and heading for higher ground in search of a connection to the outside world.

I hoped cell phone service would be restored by the time we woke up this morning, rendering Hannah and Rachel's trek into the wilderness unnecessary. I convinced myself the repaired 5G network would flood our phones with a flurry of unread text messages, emails, and social media updates. I was sure the accompanying cacophony of chimes and dings would wake us. It didn't happen.

There's still no cell service, no landline, and no internet. And, if it weren't for solar power and generators, we wouldn't have electricity either.

I'm exhausted and thankful that the spa makes a decent cup of coffee. Instead of being lulled to sleep by the peace and tranquility of our soundless surroundings, I tossed and turned all night, kept awake by the blaring silence. It's amazing how loud the world is when there's no sound.

"I miss the fridge," Connie muses, starting a new row on the shawl she's knitting and interrupting my introspection as if she can read my mind. "I never realized how the constant drone of the fridge helped me sleep." She fixes her gaze on something in the distance and smiles. "I think I use the fridge to tune out Archie's snoring." She laughs.

"For me it's the ceiling fan," I commiserate, knitting stitch after stitch on my washcloth without looking.

Eric insists on using the ceiling fan at night. It annoyed me at first, but the reliable hum of its motor has become my unchosen lullaby. I even turn it on when he's not there because the motor and light breeze lull me to sleep.

Last night, spa employees went room-to-room to check on everyone and do another informal headcount.

They asked guests to conserve as much energy as possible overnight and not waste the precious stored solar power and generators.

Connie, Hannah, and I complied. We turned off and unplugged everything in our suite. The silence was deafening. We even unplugged the motion-sensitive nightlight in the bathroom because we weren't sure if it sucked up electricity just being plugged in, or if it only uses electricity when it senses motion and turns on. Hannah offered to solve the mystery by searching the internet until she remembered we have no internet.

My brain kept tricking me into believing our connection to the outside world had been restored. Every time I was on the cusp of drifting off, my eyes would burst open, and I would raise my head, certain I heard my phone. I forced my bleary eyes to focus on the phone on the nightstand until realizing my restless brain was playing a cruel joke on my exhausted body. The phantom dinging and buzzing jolted me out of near-sleep until just before dawn.

When I wasn't listening for signs that the outside world still existed, I obsessed over Summer's death. I pictured her lifeless body in vivid detail, even recalling the chill of the cold floor tiles on my knees through my leggings, and how the dark green flecks in Summer's regurgitated smoothie contrasted against the light-green splatters. My mind's eye recreated the anguish on Autumn's face when Twyla told her that her twin had died, and the horrible retching sound that came out of

Billie when she vomited in the trash can. It was an eventful night inside my head.

"Can I get you ladies anything else?" the server asks, collecting dirty dishes from our table.

"No, thank you," Connie replies. "We'll just finish our coffee, then we'll get out of your hair."

"No hurry," the server says, balancing a tower of dirty plates on her forearm. "Take all the time you need."

"Actually," I pipe in, "I read Nadira's impressive biography yesterday, and I'd love to try her famous crispy tofu with maple-soy glaze served over jasmine rice. Do you know if it will be on today's lunch or dinner menu? Or what other tofu dishes might be on today's menu?"

Sipping her coffee, Connie glares at me over the rim like I'm sprouting a second head.

"I'm afraid not," the server replies, bending her knees and leaning back to offset the tower of dishes balanced on her forearm. "Our tofu shipment didn't arrive. We are fresh out of tofu."

"Fresh?" I clarify. "As in, if I'd ordered it yesterday it would have been available?"

"No," she shakes her head. "We haven't had tofu all week." She nods toward the floor-to-ceiling window. "Our next grocery delivery is Tuesday. If the road is fixed by then."

She smiles. We smile. Then she walks toward the kitchen surprisingly fast, considering the swaying tower of dishes she's carrying.

"Since when do you eat tofu?" Connie demands, picking up her knitting from her lap. "In twenty years, I've never seen you raise a forkful of tofu to your mouth. I don't think I've seen you within arm's reach of a piece of tofu."

"You're right," I confirm. "I can't stand tofu. I was testing a theory."

"A tofu theory?"

"A lying theory."

"Whose lie?"

"Chef Nadira Patel."

"Did our server prove or disprove your theory, my dear?"

"She proved it," I reply, finishing a row of knit stitches. "I think Nadira lied to me."

I explain to Connie how April and I saw Autumn and Nadira arguing yesterday because Autumn accused the chef of intentionally serving her chicken instead of tofu.

"Later, Nadira visited our table. She told us it was an honest mistake. She said she mixed them up because the chicken and tofu were both cubed and in similar bowls."

"How could she confuse chicken with tofu if there's no tofu?" Connie asks.

"Exactly," I reply. "Her remorse seemed genuine, but something didn't feel right about her admission."

"It's hard to fathom a chef of her calibre making such a mistake," Connie agrees.

"And when Autumn shouted at her, and threatened

to ruin her reputation, Nadira didn't flinch. She didn't argue or even defend herself. She just stood there and took it. No smile or frown. She was composed and patient. At the time, I thought her reaction reflected her professionalism. But, considering what happened after the blackout, I wonder if I misinterpreted her stoicism for smugness."

"You think Nadira served chicken to Autumn on purpose?" Connie asks. "To what end? Why would she serve chicken to someone who didn't want it?"

"That's what I'd like to find out," I reply, shoving my knitting inside my bag.

Connie leans across the table, and I lean toward her, meeting her halfway.

"Do you think the chicken scandal has something to do with Summer's death?" Connie whispers.

"I'm not sure," I admit. "Maybe it's a coincidence, or maybe Nadira took revenge on the wrong twin."

Connie straightens her back and returns to her side of the table, folding her knitting and packing it into her bag.

"If you give a baby a hammer, the entire world becomes a nail," she says.

"What?" I ask, confused and mildly concerned about Connie's mental state. "What do babies and hammers have to do with tofu or Summer's death?"

"You're the baby, my dear. When you hear about a murder, you second-guess everyone. You re-analyze what they say and how they say it. Everyone becomes a suspect."

"I can't help myself," I confess. "Is it too much?"

"Not at all, my dear." Connie lifts her coffee mug. "The world needs more babies with hammers." She pauses her mug halfway to her mouth. "Metaphorically, of course."

And with that weird, yet logical comparison, Connie sips the rest of the coffee from her mug.

CHAPTER 11

CONNIE, Hannah, and I had booked time in the hydrotherapy pools and saunas this morning. But the hydrotherapy pools are closed because of the power failure—filtering the water and maintaining the temperature would drain the spa's power reserves—and the saunas are off limits because of Summer's untimely demise. They offered us a variety of alternatives. Hannah went hiking with Rachel, and Connie and I chose a yoga class followed by guided meditation. The yoga class and guided meditation don't take as much time as the hydrotherapy pools and saunas. Between breakfast and lunch, we find ourselves with time on our hands and walk to the parking lot.

I want to make sure my car didn't suffer any storm damage. Also, we hope to tune into a local radio station for a news update about last night's storm and the road situation.

There are no local satellite stations. The only local

station we can pick up is an AM station that plays non-stop country music hits from the eighties and nineties. We sit in the car with our knitting and listen, but the top of the hour comes and goes with no weather or news updates. When the opening bars of Achy Breaky Heart start for the third time, we give up and head back to the main building.

We take our time and explore the grounds, taking full advantage of the beautiful spring day. The sun is bright, and birds serenade us. A gentle breeze wafts through the budding trees and long wild grasses that line the perimeter of the property. Tulips and daffodils reach for the blue, cloudless sky from the cultivated beds that punctuate the well-groomed grounds and created walking path. Besides a few downed branches and snapped stems, there's no evidence that Mother Nature ripped through here last night in a vicious rage, stealing a police cruiser and leaving chaos, a lack of modern amenities, and death in her wake.

On the west side of the main building, we discover a large deck with lounge chairs and cozy sitting areas overlooking the breathtaking view.

"We must come out here at sunset," Connie comments. "It would be beautiful!"

"It's beautiful now," I respond.

The vast deck extends the entire length of the building and features chamfered deck boards that create the illusion the deck winds and undulates like the natural scenery that surrounds it.

Several doors exit onto the deck. The door that says,

Sauna gets my attention. I squint to read the sign on the next door. *Ladies Change Room*. The next door reads, *Massage Therapy*. Inside, the sauna and massage therapy area are separated by the change room. Outside, their emergency exits are only a few feet apart.

Architecture is a mystery to me, but if Autumn got a hot stone massage while Summer was in the sauna, she would have been seconds away when Summer died.

Did Autumn use the emergency exits to sneak in and out of the sauna and kill her sister? The thought sends a shiver up my spine. Until now, it never occurred to me that Autumn might be a suspect in her twin's death. But, as Eric says, everyone is a suspect until they're eliminated.

"Where shall we sit, my dear?" Connie asks, bringing me back to the here and now. "Sun or shade?"

Guests dot the chairs and tables. Some chat in small groups, some sit alone with a book, and some relax with their faces aimed at the sun.

We scope out the seating situation, and spot two empty loungers, side-by-side.

"Over there," I reply, pointing to the loungers on the far side of the deck.

We weave through the chairs and tables, and I keep my stare affixed on our destination until a delicate sneeze distracts me.

"Bless you," I say, stopping to look down at the source of the sneeze. Her face is obscured by a wide-brimmed sun hat, but I recognize the woman and am surprised to find her sitting here by herself. "Autumn?"

She lifts the floppy brim of her hat to see who said her name.

"Hello," she says. "Megan, right?"

"Right," I reply. "And this is Connie." I gesture next to me.

Connie extends her hand and offers Autumn her condolences.

It's difficult to assess how Autumn is coping the day after her twin sister's death. Between the wide brim hat and large sunglasses, I can't make out her expression. But if her slumped shoulders, dipped chin, and deflated demeanour are any indication, she's not doing well. And who can blame her?

"Are you alone?" I ask. "Where is Billie?"

Is it presumptuous to assume that Billie would be with her? Using my relationship with April as a standard for comparison, I can't imagine leaving April alone for even one second after such a loss.

"She's here," Autumn replies, gesturing around her. "Somewhere. She's not feeling well this morning and rushed inside. Again. She'll be back any minute."

"Billie wasn't feeling well last night, either," I remark, having graphic flashbacks of Billie's physical reaction after she learned about Summer's death.

"She's struggling with Summer's death," Autumn remarks. "The three of us have a long, complicated relationship. It can't be easy for her to be best friends with twins. Sometimes Billie would get jealous of the bond my sister and I shared. She doesn't like to admit it, but I know she felt like a third wheel sometimes. Especially lately."

I'm about to ask Autumn what she means by *especially lately* when Connie changes the subject.

"Well, why don't we join you until your friend returns, hmm?"

"Unless, of course, you want to be alone," I add. "We'd love to sit with you but we don't want to impose."

"And you won't offend us if you say no," Connie says.

Autumn hesitates before she answers, glancing around her. I assume she's sizing up her options or searching for an excuse to decline our offer.

"That would be great," she responds, a hint of a smile on her pursed lips.

Connie and I claim the lounge chair next to Autumn's. We sit on it sideways as if it were a backless sofa. We pull out our knitting and start stitching.

"You're a suspect, you know," Autumn says curtly and out of nowhere.

"Excuse me?"

I place my knitting in my lap and give Autumn my undivided attention.

"Megan is a suspect in your sister's death?" Connie asks in a whisper, checking our immediate surroundings for eavesdroppers.

Autumn nods and turns toward me. I assume she's looking at me but can't tell for sure because I can't see her eyes behind her dark glasses.

"You and your tall blonde friend are suspects," she says like it's no big deal.

"April?" I ask, dumbfounded.

"If that's your tall blonde friend's name," Autumn replies.

Twyla thinks April and I killed Summer?

CHAPTER 12

"Did Twyla tell you April and I are suspects?

Waiting for her answer, my body freezes. I hold my breath, and I swear, even my heart stops beating for fear that any bodily function will interfere with my ability to hear her response.

"She didn't say you *aren't* suspects, if you know what I mean."

"I know exactly what you mean." I nod, after untangling her double negative.

Twyla seemed skeptical about my responses to every question she asked me. Sensing her misgivings, I tried extra hard to appear honest and forthcoming. My aggressive efforts to convince her might have led Twyla to believe I have something to hide.

I add a visit with Twyla to my mental do list.

"Don't worry," Autumn continues. "I know you and your friend had nothing to do with my sister's death."

"We didn't," I assure her. "But how do you know

that? If you know it wasn't us, you must have a suspect in mind."

"Oh, I know who killed Summer," Autumn states, sitting up straight and exhibiting the same outspoken confidence she had when she argued with Nadira about the chicken-tofu mix-up. "The chef did it."

"You believe Nadira killed your sister?" Connie asks.

"I don't believe she did," Autumn clarifies. "I know she did."

"How?" I ask.

"She tried to poison me yesterday," Autumn explains. "And I confronted her. Nadira knows I know she intended to kill me. Summer wasn't her target, I was. She killed the wrong twin."

I'm not sure if serving someone the wrong protein qualifies as attempted murder, but since I already suspect Nadira is lying about the chicken-tofu fiasco, I'm open to Autumn's theory.

"That's a big accusation, Autumn," I say.

"If she didn't do it, then where was she when my sister died?" Autumn asks, emotion catching the last word of her question. "No one will tell me where Nadira was when Summer died. She won't talk to me. Twyla won't tell me anything. If Nadira was innocent, wouldn't she shout her alibi from the rooftop of this place?"

She makes a good point. But just because Autumn can't verify Nadira's alibi, doesn't mean Nadira killed Summer. And just because Nadira served Autumn chicken instead of tofu doesn't mean she was trying to poison Autumn.

"My sister was a good person." Autumn's voice is thick with emotion. "I don't mean she was a good person the same way everyone says their deceased loved one was a good person. My sister really was a good person. She was brave. She made sacrifices other people would never make."

"Like what?" I ask, wondering if Summer donated an organ, or devoted her life to a worthy cause, or something.

"When we were eighteen," Autumn begins, "Summer had a part-time job at a local bar. One night, she witnessed a murder in the parking lot. Instead of looking the other way, she did the right thing and cooperated with the police. Her testimony put a killer behind bars and got justice for the victim's family."

"That certainly was a selfless act," Connie agrees. "Your sister sounds like an upstanding person. Your family must be very proud of her."

"I am her family. Summer and I didn't have anyone else. Now that she's dead, I'm all alone. That's what makes her actions so selfless. The murder my sister witnessed was committed by a mob boss's son. My sister risked her life to testify against him. For her safety, and for ours, she went into witness protection. They relocated her. They gave her a new name and new identity. To keep us safe, Summer couldn't have any contact with me or our mum. She was all alone for over ten years."

"She must not be in witness protection anymore, if she was here with you," I surmise. "What happened? Why did she come back?"

"The killer she helped convict died last year. His father, the mob boss, died a few months later. Summer felt safe enough to come back. The authorities agreed that the threat to Summer's safety was minimal since the killer and his father had died. But it was too late. Our mother passed away three years ago." A single tear streams down Autumn's cheek, and she takes a moment to compose herself. "Summer did not know our mother had died. She gave up everything to keep us safe. She gave up her life for us twice. First when she went into hiding, and again when she abandoned her new life and came home."

"Autumn, could your sister's testimony against the killer have anything to do with her death?" I ask.

"No," Autumn replies shaking her head, tears streaming down her cheeks from behind her glasses. "She'd only been back for a few months, and she laid low. Not many people knew she had left witness protection. Since the killer and his father died, the organized crime family fell apart. There was no one alive who wanted Summer dead. Even the authorities agreed it was safe for Summer to come home. Anyway, no one knew we would be here this week, except me, Billie, and Summer. Billie booked it a few days before we checked in."

"Did you accept the hot stone massage they offered

you two in the change room yesterday?" I ask, hoping to establish Autumn's alibi.

"No. I offered it to Summer," Autumn replies. "I had the early symptoms of a migraine. I went upstairs for an early night."

"Summer had the hot stone massage?" I ask, confused because Summer died in the sauna.

"No," Autumn replies. "She wanted to go to the saunas. Summer loved the saunas. We've visited them every day since we checked in. Billie took the hot stone massage."

"I see."

I glance at the emergency exit doors. If Autumn is telling the truth, Billie was near Summer around the time Summer died. Well, Billie's emergency exit was next to Summer's emergency exit.

I sit up straight and squeeze my shoulder blades together.

"Are you all right, my dear?" Connie asks.

"Nothing a hot stone massage won't help," I reply, then turn my attention back to Autumn.

"When Summer was in the sauna, and Billie got a massage, you were in your room?"

"That's right," Autumn confirms. "Fighting migraine symptoms caused by the chicken Nadira tried to poison me with."

"Why did you visit the front desk last night?" I ask.

"I stopped at the front desk and asked Maria for ibuprofen."

"Did she give you some?"

"Yes, but it didn't help."

"How is your head today?" Connie asks.

"A dull throb," Autumn responds. "My whole body is a dull, achy throb. It's the only thing I've felt since Summer died. Dull and achy."

"When did you realize Summer was missing?" I ask.

"When the power went out. Summer and Billie didn't come back to the room. I went downstairs to find them."

"Did you find them?" Connie asks.

"No," Autumn replies, shaking her head. "I went upstairs again in case they returned to the room, and we missed each other. Our room was empty. I tried to text them, but my cell phone wasn't working."

"Did you stay in the room and wait for them?" Connie asks.

"I couldn't sit around doing nothing when I didn't know where Summer and Billie were," Autumn explains, somewhat defensively. "I was on my way downstairs to search for them again when an employee asked me to join the rest of the guests and staff in the bistro for a storm update. She said spa treatments were cancelled, and everyone should proceed to the bistro."

"But you weren't in the bistro," I remind her. "You came in late, searching for Summer."

"I waited outside," Autumn explains. "You just didn't see me in the crowd. I watched the door for Summer and Billie. I assumed they were together and on their way like everyone else."

"But Billie was late," I point out. "She arrived partway through Maria and Twyla's update."

"I know," Autumn agrees. "She didn't see me in the hall when she slipped into the bistro alone. I panicked when Summer wasn't with her." She grabs her gut. "I had a bad feeling. Summer and I used to call it twintuition. I knew something was wrong. I knew Summer was in trouble."

"What did you do?" Connie asked.

"I ran back upstairs to check the room. Empty. Then I went toward the change room, but it was dark and abandoned. I assumed no one was there and ran to the bistro. I had hoped Summer was there, and I had missed her."

"But you didn't," I say.

"I didn't," Autumn concurs. "Summer wasn't there. She wasn't anywhere."

"There you are!" Billie exclaims, approaching us from behind Autumn's lounge chair. "You moved while I was inside."

Billie climbs over the chair and joins Autumn in the generous lounger. Autumn wriggles over to accommodate her friend.

"Sorry," Autumn says to her friend. "A chair in the shade came available, so I jumped at it. I would have texted you, but you know..." She holds up her useless cell phone and shrugs.

"Well," I say, smiling and stuffing my knitting inside my knitting bag, "now that Billie is back, we'll get out of your way."

Connie and I stand up.

"Please don't leave on my account," Billie says. "I think I'm coming down with something. If I hurry inside again, it's a relief to know Autumn won't be alone."

Connie and I sit back down and pull out our knitting again.

Autumn stands and dusts nothing from the front of her navy Capri pants.

"I was about to head upstairs, anyway. My migraine is making a comeback."

"I'll come with you," Billie offers, jumping to her feet.

"It's OK, Billie," Autumn insists. "I'd like to be alone. I'm not very good company right now."

"If you're sure," Billie says. "I'll come upstairs and check on you in a while. In the meantime, there is an employee near the stairs. They have walkie-talkies now, so they can call the front desk if you need anything."

Autumn thanks her, then she thanks us. She hitches her canvas tote bag on her shoulder and drops her book and cell phone inside. She takes one step away from the lounge chair and collides head-on with another guest, also wearing a wide-brimmed sunhat and large sunglasses. Victims of their valiant attempts to avoid sun damage.

"*Ooof,*" the guest says, flailing her arms to stay upright.

"Sorry," Autumn mutters, stumbling backward.

Billie catches Autumn by the arm and navigates a

controlled fall onto the lounge chair, and with the reflexes of someone half her age, Connie grasps the other guest around the waist and holds her steady while she regains her balance.

Both women are uninjured, but amid the commotion, their bags slip off their respective shoulders, landing upside down on the lounge chair and deck. Connie and I abandon our knitting, and the five of us drop to the ground, scrabbling to collect their commingled belongings before they roll away.

Grabbing at the scattered items, the mystery woman's sunglasses fall off her face.

"Hi," I say to the doctor.

The doctor's beige linen culottes and linen tunic match her sunhat and her beige tote bag with leather handles.

"Oh! Hello, again," she replies, replacing her sunglasses.

"It's you," Autumn says when she realizes who the woman is.

"It's me," the doctor replies.

While Autumn and the doctor exchange awkward pleasantries, we take turns holding out the items we recovered from the ground. Each woman claims their belongings by plucking them from our open hands. A guest from a nearby table returns a lip balm that rolled all the way to her chair, and another guest returns a pharmacy receipt that blew into her lap.

"I think we're sorted!" says the doctor.

"Again, I'm sorry!" Autumn says, assessing the

contents of her canvas tote bag. "I'm tired and distracted today."

They exchange more apologies, and when they're both satisfied that they're sufficiently sorry and sufficiently forgiven, the doctor continues on her way, and Autumn continues to her room.

As Autumn leaves, a glint of amber plastic under a nearby chair catches my eye. I lunge for it. A prescription bottle with Autumn's name on it. *Lasmiditan*, according to the label.

"Autumn!" I shout.

She turns, and I hold up the pill bottle, shaking it. She starts back toward me, and I walk toward her, meeting her partway.

"Thank you," she says, taking the bottle from me. "These are my migraine meds. I don't know how I'd cope without them." She slips the bottle into her bag.

"If you have migraine medication, why did you ask for ibuprofen at the front desk?" I ask.

For a split second, she freezes, then nods.

"The migraine pills are great," she explains. "But they have side effects. I feel dizzy and drowsy for a day after I take them. I use over-the-counter medication or natural remedies first and rely on the prescription as a last resort." She lets out a long sigh. "Today might be a last resort day." Autumn pats the side of her bag.

CHAPTER 13

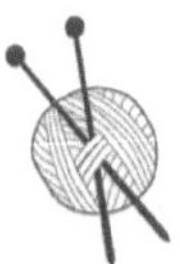

BACK AT THE LOUNGE CHAIR, Connie and Billie are deep in conversation.

"Billie was just saying she's worried about how Autumn is coping with Summer's death," Connie says. "Apparently Autumn is not herself."

"It's true," Billie admits, her eyes searching mine for something. Sympathy? Compassion? Understanding? "Autumn has hardly said a word since Summer died. I've never seen her like this, not even after their mum died."

"Twins share a special connection the rest of us can't understand," Connie reminds her.

"It's more than that." Billie bites her lip, her eyes darting in random directions, like she's struggling to find the right words. "You don't understand," she says, bouncing her knee and tapping the lounge chair cush-ion. "She's too… too… quiet."

"Can you give us an example?" I ask, trying to help her express herself.

Billie takes a deep breath, counting to four on her fingers. Then she holds it while she counts to four on her other hand.

"One... two... three... four..." Billie counts as she exhales. She looks me in the eye. "Autumn is not a quiet woman. I've known her since kindergarten. Autumn doesn't turn her emotions inward, she works through her feelings out loud. If she's sad, she cries and talks about why she's sad. When she's happy, she laughs and tells everyone why she's happy. If she's angry, she shouts and complains until she figures out how to fix it."

"Like she shouted and complained to Nadira about the chicken?" I ask.

"Yes!" Billie agrees, letting out a sigh of relief. "What if Summer's death is too much for her? What if Autumn is quiet because she's having a breakdown?"

"Maybe Autumn isn't processing her feelings out loud because she can't," Connie suggests, squeezing Billie's knee. "It's been less than twenty-four hours since Summer died. Autumn might still be in shock. Summer's death blindsided her."

"Connie's right," I add. "It's possible Autumn doesn't know how she feels yet. Or she's denying her feelings, so she can function until it's safe to get out of here."

"You're probably right," Billie concedes. "Autumn

must feel like part of herself died, and that's gotta be hard to process."

"I can't imagine what she's going through," Connie sympathizes.

"How do I help her?" Billie asks. "Usually, I listen and sympathize. But how can I listen if Autumn won't talk?"

"Just be here," I reply. "She knows you're here to listen when she's ready."

"How are you coping with Summer's death?" Connie asks. "Autumn told us the three of you were a tight unit. This must be hard for you too."

"It is," Billie admits. "I have so many feelings. Sadness, shock, guilt, disbelief."

"Which emotion is causing your tummy trouble?" I ask, wondering why Billie feels guilty.

"Megan said you weren't well when you found out about Summer, and Autumn said you've been sick again today," Connie adds.

"I'm not sure the nausea has anything to do with Summer's death. I felt like this before she died. It started when we got here." Billie looks around for anyone listening nearby, then leans in closer to Connie and me. "I think it's the food," she whispers. "Nothing I've eaten here agrees with me. I know Nadira has won awards, and everyone raves about how talented she is, but her food doesn't agree with me."

"Oh," Connie says, rubbing her stomach in sympathy, "That's unfortunate."

"Did you mention your issues to Nadira?" I ask.

"No," Billie replies, "Autumn did. She's the one who pointed out that I was fine until I started eating here."

"What did Autumn say to Nadira?" I ask.

"Which time?" Billie asks. "Autumn kicked up a fuss every time I had a bout of nausea. She kept a list of everything I'd eaten and looked for common foods that might cause it. She's convinced Nadira uses secret ingredients that make me sick. Autumn has suffered with migraines most of her life. She's a big believer that what we eat affects our bodies. She's so desperate to keep the migraines away that she's tried more elimination diets than I can count."

"Is that why she's pescatarian?" Connie asks.

"Yes," Billie confirms. "Through elimination diets, Autumn determined that red meat, poultry, and pork contribute to her migraines. She's been pescatarian for almost a year, and she's very diligent about it. She also avoids refined sugar and dairy."

"So, yesterday's altercation with Nadira about the chicken-tofu confusion wasn't their first argument?" I ask.

"No," Billie replies. "But Autumn doesn't like to call it arguing. She prefers to call it *advocating*. Autumn is a dedicated advocate. She confronted Nadira after every meal that made me nauseous." She shrugs. "So pretty much after every meal I've had here. I asked her not to. I told her I don't want my stomach issues to interfere with our vacation, but Autumn insisted. She said I'm too sick to advocate for myself."

"How did Nadira respond when Autumn accused her of not disclosing ingredients?" Connie asks.

"She denied it," Billie replies. "At first she was offended because Autumn attacked her integrity. Nadira said withholding ingredient information would be unethical and dangerous. She said she accommodates every guest's dietary needs."

"At first?" I ask.

"I think she was fed up with Autumn's constant advocating. She stopped arguing and just stood there, nodding until Autumn finished."

"That must've frustrated Autumn," I suggest.

"It did," Billie confirms. "And it made her more determined. She threatened to warn people. She said she would leave bad reviews, warn food bloggers, and ruin Nadira's career."

Earlier, Autumn mentioned they checked in on Wednesday. If she advocated on behalf of Billie after every meal, that's at least nine confrontations. Nine times she accused Nadira of making a guest sick. Ten times if we include the tofu-chicken scandal. Did Autumn's constant complaints and accusations push Nadira over the edge? Could Autumn be on to something with her theory that Nadira killed the wrong twin?

"There you are!" April calls, weaving through the chairs with Tamara, Rachel, and Hannah in tow.

"Hi," Connie and I say in unison.

"You remember Billie, right?" I say to April as I gesture to Billie.

"Of course," April replies smiling. "I'm so sorry about Summer."

April joins Billie on her lounger. Rachel, having inherited April's impossibly long legs, steps over the lounger with the same effort it would take me to step over a sidewalk crack and sits next to April. Connie and I squeeze together to make room for Tamara and Hannah on our lounger. It's snug, but we make it work.

April introduces Billie to everyone.

"Rachel and I just saw Autumn," Hannah informs Billie. "We went upstairs to drop off our antennae, and Maria was letting Autumn into her room because Autumn lost her key."

"She did?" Connie asks, squeezing her eyebrows together and pausing her needles mid-stitch. "I distinctly remember picking up a room key when Autumn and the doctor collided. The doctor took the key out of my hand."

"Are you sure?" Billie asks. "Because I picked up a room key too, and the doctor insisted it was hers and took it."

"It sounds like the doctor accidentally took both keys," I conclude.

"At least we know who has it," Connie says. "I'm sure Maria will find the doctor and get Autumn's key back."

As Hannah and Rachel tell us about their fruitless search for 5G service, Billie's complexion blanches. The skin around her eyes darkens, and her eyes appear more sunken than a moment ago. I hope it's not because we went from three people to seven people crammed on two lounge chairs. Despite the generous size of the lounge chairs, it's a tight fit.

"I hear you had a hot stone massage last night," I say to Billie, hoping to verify her alibi and distract her from her obvious discomfort. "How was it? I'm thinking of booking one."

"I can't say," Billie answers, then swallows hard. "The massage therapist was just getting started when the power went out." She swipes the back of her hand across her forehead and wipes it on the thigh of her grey leggings. "It was too dark to finish the massage, and the stones need electricity to stay warm. I got dressed, and the massage therapist and I left."

"Did you leave through the emergency exit, or the main door?" I ask, pointing to the emergency exit.

"The main door." Billie struggles to swallow, flaring her nostrils. "The massage therapist turned off the lights and locked up behind us."

"Did anyone else see today's lunch menu?" Tamara asks. "Today's special is one of Nadira's specialties, Zucchini Roshti Yucca Burger with French Mustard Dressing."

As we *mmm* and discuss how yummy and intriguing it sounds, Billie clutches her book with trembling hands. Her knuckles are white. She stands up.

"I'm sorry," Billie says. "I don't feel well." She clasps a hand over her mouth and navigates away from the crowded lounge chairs.

"Is there anything we can do?" Connie asks.

"Mmm-mmm," Billie hums, her hand still covering her mouth. "No thank you," she mumbles, striding away.

"Is she OK?" Hannah asks.

"I hope it wasn't something we said," Tamara adds, taking advantage of the space freed up by Billie's departure and switching lounge chairs.

"She's had tummy trouble for the last few days," I explain.

"She certainly looked like she wasn't feeling well," Connie observes. "Did you notice how quickly the colour drained from her face?"

"And she had beads of sweat on her forehead and upper lip," April adds. "It's not hot enough to sweat that much."

"Especially since we're sitting in the shade." Connie points her knitting needle at the overhead awning.

If Billie was with the massage therapist when the power went out, and they left together like she claims, why was she late getting to the Epicurean Bistro last night? She crept in more than halfway through Maria's update. Where was Billie between leaving the massage and showing up at the bistro? Could she have gone back to her room? Autumn said their room was empty. But Autumn left twice to search for Summer and Billie. Is it possible they missed each other?

"What's this?" April asks, producing a sandwich-size freezer bag from the crack where the back and bottom lounge cushions meet. "Is it yours?"

She looks back and forth from me to Connie, dangling the clear plastic baggie between her fingers.

"It's not mine," I say, shoving my knitting inside my knitting bag.

"It's not mine either," Connie confirms.

I reach out to take the baggie.

Hannah and Connie lean in to inspect the baggie with me. It's a collection of leaf clippings. I smush them around between the plastic sides of the bag, spreading them out and inspecting them.

"It looks like someone chopped up leaves or grass," Connie says.

The angular, straight edges on the non-uniform clippings look like someone used scissors to chop the leaves, or grass, or whatever this is into small, random-sized pieces.

"Why would someone chop them up?" I ask, turning the bag to inspect the contents from the other side.

"To smoke it?" Tamara suggests, shrugging one shoulder.

"You think it's weed?" I ask, bringing the bag to my face for a closer look. "Maybe it fell out of Autumn's bag. I've heard of people using weed to treat migraines."

"It doesn't look like weed," Hannah comments over my shoulder.

"How would you know?" I ask, narrowing my eyes on my daughter and raising one eyebrow.

"From the drug awareness campaigns and anti-drug posters at school," she counters with a smug grin.

"Hannah's right," Connie says. "These don't look like marijuana leaves." She pulls herself upright. "These leaves are fresh." She gestures to the baggie on my lap. "Marijuana leaves are dried."

"I see." I redirect my narrowed gaze to Connie. "How do you know about drying out marijuana leaves?"

"That's what I've heard," she replies sheepishly, fidgeting with her knitting and mumbling something about common knowledge.

April reaches across and takes the baggie.

"This piece has scalloped edges," she says, sliding the plastic between her thumb and forefinger until she separates and traps a larger piece. "It looks like parsley."

Tamara leans over her wife's shoulder for a closer look at the mystery leaves.

"Wild parsley is pretty common where we live. Or maybe the spa has an herb garden, and a parsley enthusiast pinched off a few stalks," I suggest.

"It's too early for wild parsley," Connie insists. "Even with the warm spring we've been having, I doubt there's much wild parsley in the mountains yet."

"Here"—I hold out my hand and April gives me the baggie—"Parsley smells like grass. I'll open the bag and sniff it."

"No!" Tamara shouts as I'm about to breach the plastic baggie's zipped seal. "Megan! Don't."

Tamara snatches the still-sealed baggie and brings it close to her face.

"I think this might be spotted water hemlock." She rolls a few pieces between the plastic. "These look like young leaves. From a young plant. And these white bits could be pieces of root." She looks up at us and blinks, refocussing her large brown eyes. "The root is the most toxic part."

"Why would someone carry around a baggie of poison?" Connie asks.

Our collective silence speaks volumes. The only reason a person would have a baggie of cut-up, poisonous leaves would be to poison someone. We all know it, but none of us wants to say it.

"I think we should give this to Twyla," I say, breaking the somber silence.

"If T is wrong, and this is just parsley, Twyla will think we're alarmists," April argues.

"T" is Tamara's nickname.

"If Mum is right, and we don't hand it in, we could be withholding evidence," Rachel counters.

"I need to visit Twyla anyway," I say standing up. "This gives me a good excuse."

"I'll come with you," Tamara offers. "I can explain why I suspect it's spotted water hemlock, and she'll see it's an educated guess and not hysterical speculation." She rubs her tummy. "Can we stop at the juice bar on the way? It's almost lunchtime, and I'm starving. I've been craving a Green Powerhouse smoothie since Hannah had one last night."

"Of course," I say.

Tamara points at April and me.

"We have to wash our hands," she instructs. "Do not touch your face or anything else until you've washed your hands with soap and water."

April nods.

I nod.

"Just having skin contact with this plant is deadly."

Hannah takes my knitting bag, so I don't touch it with my unwashed hands, then she, Connie, April, and Rachel follow us to the door.

Never in my life has my nose been as itchy as it is since Tamara ordered me not to touch my face.

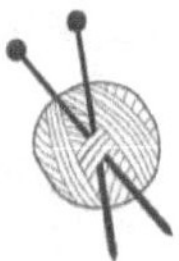

CHAPTER 14

"How do you know so much about spotted water hemlock?" I ask Tamara while the juice bar attendant makes her smoothie.

"My mother is a botanist," Tamara replies.

"Oh, I thought she worked in the food industry."

"She did," Tamara clarifies. "She researched genetically modified edible plants."

"Well, I'm glad your mother shared her botanical knowledge with you. You just saved my life. If it weren't for you, I would've sniffed those leaves and picked them up with my bare hands too."

"Before my mum worked for the food company, she worked in the agricultural industry. Spotted water hemlock was a problem for local farmers. The plant spread and grew faster than farmers could eradicate it. Livestock would eat it and die. That's why it's also known as *cowbane*. My mum was part of a team that tried to find a large-scale solution to the spotted water hemlock problem. That's why I know so much." She shrugs. "She would talk about her work, and there were photos of it lying around our house."

"Lucky for me, your mother brought her work home with her."

The juice bar attendant hands Tamara a Green Powerhouse smoothie and a straw. I offer to carry the wad of paper towels, so she has both hands free to enjoy her drink.

On our way to the juice bar, we stopped at the bathroom to wash our hands. The first thing I did with my clean hands was scratch the tip of my nose. It was the most satisfying nose scratch of my life. The next thing I did was take photos of the suspicious baggie with my cell phone. Then Tamara wrapped the baggie in a wad of paper towels to reduce the likelihood of oils or trace amounts of spotted water hemlock transferring to someone's hands from the outside of the baggie.

On our way to the front desk to ask for Twyla, I tell Tamara what Autumn said about April and me making Twyla's suspect list.

"That's ridiculous," Tamara says. "If you and April killed Summer, why would you lead the police to her body? And why would you kill Summer, anyway? You guys didn't know her, and you have no motive. April and you have alibis. You were at the front desk when Summer died. April was with me and Rachel, then she went downstairs for a smoothie and ran into you."

"I know," I say. "But Twyla has to assume everybody is a suspect until she proves otherwise."

"Then we'll help her prove otherwise," Tamara declares, then sips her smoothie.

"This weekend was supposed to be about spending quality time together, relaxing, and pampering ourselves. We weren't supposed to find a dead body in the aftermath of a storm and solve the murder to prove our innocence."

"It can be two things." Tamara shrugs and sips her smoothie again.

"I regret not getting one," I say, watching the green liquid travel through the white straw. "Is it good?"

"Mmm-hmm," Tamara says, nodding and sipping the green liquid through the straw. "Want to try?"

We stop walking and Tamara offers me the clear plastic cup. I take it and use the straw to stir the green contents. Thicker than water, but not as thick as a triple thick milkshake. I bring the straw to my lips and take a small sip.

"Yummy," I say, then take a bigger sip. "It tastes better than it looks." I hold the cup at my eye level. "Where are the dark green flecks?"

"What dark green flecks?" Tamara asks, taking back the cup. She holds it at her eye level and inspects the contents. "Is there supposed to be dark green flecks?"

"I think so," I reply. "Summer's Green Powerhouse smoothie was the same colour as yours, but with dark green flecks."

"Are you sure?" Tamara asks. "Hannah's smoothie didn't have dark green flecks. It looked like this one." She holds up her cup like she's making a toast. "She let me taste it, and I didn't see any dark green flecks or taste any chunks."

I unlock my phone and find the photos I took at the crime scene last night.

"See," I say, showing Tamara the photo of the regurgitated smoothie. I pinch the screen and zoom in. "Dark green flecks."

"Weird," Tamara says. "Those are probably bits of lettuce that were in Summer's stomach."

We resume walking, and I think back to last night and the dark-green flecks in Summer's smoothie. Did bits of salad come up with the smoothie when she threw up? Did Summer customize her smoothie? Was it a Green Powerhouse smoothie, or something else from the juice bar menu? I'm certain she said it was a Green Powerhouse smoothie when Hannah and I talked to the twins in the change room. As I contemplate the scene in sauna three last night, and the green flecks in Summer's smoothie, I stare at the wad of paper towel in my hand.

Then it hits me.

I freeze on the spot and gasp.

"What is it?" Tamara asks. "What's wrong?" She brings the straw to her lips.

"Tamara, no!"

As she closes her lips around the tip of the straw, I slam the smoothie cup out of her hand. We both leap back as it crashes to the wood floor, splattering light green smoothie everywhere. No dark green flecks.

"What the heck, Megan?!" Tamara looks at her

empty hand, then at the mess on the floor. "That was a good smoothie!"

"I'm sorry, T," I plead. "But I'm positive that Summer's smoothie had dark green flecks."

"And?" Tamara urges, unsatisfied with my justification for destroying her smoothie and making an enormous mess.

"It just occurred to me that if Summer's smoothie was the only Green Powerhouse smoothie with dark green flecks, maybe the dark green flecks didn't belong in the smoothie."

As if we choreographed it, our eyes shift from each other to the wad of paper towels in my hand.

"What if the murderer put spotted water hemlock in Summer's smoothie?" Tamara ruminates, arriving at the same conclusion I reached just before I smacked her drink away from her face. We look up and our eyes meet. "That means Summer's killer dropped the baggie."

"Or planted it when they snuck out of the emergency exit after they killed Summer," I suggest. "But we don't know for sure that the leaves are spotted water hemlock. We might be jumping to a lot of conclusions."

"I'm over ninety percent sure it's spotted water hemlock," Tamara admits with a sigh. "I'd know for certain from the smell, but I'm scared to sniff it because I can't remember if the smell is toxic."

"And we don't have internet access to check," I say, finishing her sentence. "What does spotted water hemlock smell like?"

"Carrots," Tamara replies. "Mum used to talk about the strong carrot smell."

"I'm sorry about your smoothie," I say. "I panicked and thought your smoothie might have dark green flecks that we couldn't see through the cup."

We squat and examine the splattered smoothie against the wood floor. Tamara drags the straw through the green liquid, searching for anything out of place. Neither of us spot anything.

"Everything all right, ladies?" asks the perky employee with the bouncy ponytail. "Uh oh... it looks like we had a little accident."

"It's my fault," I admit. "I'm sorry. Sometimes I swear my fingers are butter."

We laugh.

"Don't worry about it," the employee assures me. "These things happen." She plucks a two-way radio from the waistband of her wrinkle-free beige uniform pants and summons a mop and bucket. "Can I have someone replace your smoothie?" she asks.

"No, thank you," Tamara replies. "It was good, but we're having lunch soon, and I don't want to fill up on smoothie."

The lie rolls off Tamara's lips as though it was the truth. But I guess the truth, that we're worried an unhinged psychopath is poisoning smoothies, would either freak out the employee or make us sound like overreacting drama queens. Dealing with paranoid guests' ridiculous-sounding conspiracy theories is probably above her pay grade.

"OK." The employee flashes us a cheery smile and re-holsters the two-way radio in her waistband. "Have a great lunch! You're in for a treat if you order Chef Nadira's Zucchini Roshti Yucca Burger."

"I know," Tamara agrees. "I can't wait. Have you tried it? Was it good?"

The peppy employee's animated review of Nadira's signature dish makes my tummy grumble. It feels like breakfast was four days ago, not four hours.

As a second employee pushing a mop and bucket on wheels approaches us, I ask both employees if they know where we can find Twyla.

"She was with Maria a while ago," replies the perky employee. "Maria will know where to find her."

"Maria's on lunch," says the employee with the mop and bucket. "She usually has lunch in her room. She'll be back in about an hour."

"Thanks," I say, smiling as Tamara takes my arm and tugs me away.

"I know where the employee rooms are," Tamara whispers as we continue down the hall arm-in-arm.

"How?" I ask.

"Last night when you and April were in the sauna, Connie and I socialized in the hall with the other guests."

"When Connie gave impromptu knitting lessons?" I ask.

"That's right," Tamara says. "She taught garter stitch to about ten people, including two employees. Connie chatted with them. You know what she's like."

"I sure do," I respond.

Connie is the most extroverted extrovert I know. She has never met a stranger and can make friends in an empty room.

"She made friends with the employees and asked them about their jobs, their love lives, their families, all of it," Tamara explains. "In the course of the conversation, the employees mentioned the staff dorm and where it's located."

"Maria's room is in the dorm?"

"No," Tamara replies. "Maria sleeps in the main building with us. Her apartment is on the first floor behind the front desk."

"If Maria is in her home, having lunch, maybe we should wait an hour and talk to her when she's on the clock."

"We won't hijack her lunch. We'll just ask where Twyla is," Tamara argues. "Nadira only serves the lunch special for a two-hour window. If we wait to talk to Maria, then talk to Twyla, we won't get any Zucchini Roshti Yucca Burger with French Mustard Dressing."

"Fine," I agree, doubting we'll get past the person at the front desk, anyway.

CHAPTER 15

THE FRONT DESK IS UNATTENDED. A guest enjoying a nearby massage chair informs us that Maria left for lunch about five minutes ago. According to the guest, the person covering the reception desk in Maria's absence was called away to deal with a spill.

"She got a call over the two-way radio about a spilled smoothie." The guest's voice warbles from the vibration of the massage chair. "She rolled out of here with the mop-and-bucket cart."

"Thanks," Tamara says, smirking at me.

The guest doesn't see Tamara's smirk because her eyes are closed. Her back arches, and she moans as the massage roller travels up her spine. I make a mental note to try the massage chairs before we check out.

"Come on," Tamara mouths, jerking her head toward the reception desk with her eyes wide.

"OK," I mouth, following her into forbidden territory.

The door behind the reception desk leads into Maria's office. Her office is neat and messy at the same time, like my house. The messy bits are confined to designated areas.

Two stacks of paper and files sit on Maria's desk. Notices about upcoming spa events and health and safety reminders are pinned to a large bulletin board behind the desk. A variety of jackets and sweaters hang from the coat rack in the corner, and the boot tray below it features a pair of winter boots, a pair of rain boots, and a pair of hiking boots arranged in order of height.

I suspect Maria created the hand-drawn chart on the whiteboard last night in a haste. It lists all the areas of the spa. Some areas, like the pool and sauna, have *x's* through them. The areas that are closed because of the storm or because of Summer's death. Other areas have employee names listed, like the ones stationed on each floor to attend to guest inquiries until the landline is fixed.

The black and gold nameplate on Maria's desk reads: *MARIA CLARK* and underneath in smaller letters, *GENERAL MANAGER.*

"So that's what the C on Maria's name tag stands for," I mutter.

Every spa employee wears a name tag on their golf-style uniform shirt. Each name tag features the employee's first name and last initial.

"Why do they bother putting last initials on the name tags?" Tamara asks as if she can read my mind.

"Why not just the first name, or the first name and full last name?"

"I guess it's useful if two employees have the same name. In case there are two Marias and you need to tell them apart?" I venture a guess.

Straight ahead of us is a closed door.

"Maria's apartment must be through here." Tamara reaches for the doorknob.

"Wait." I place my hand on her arm. "We should knock. What if this door opens into Maria's personal space? What if we walk in on her watching TV in her underwear and eating cereal?"

"That's unlikely," Tamara replies with a chuckle. "We're still using generators. There's no way Maria would waste power to watch TV."

That's the biggest concern Tamara took from my hypothetical scenario? Tamara raps her knuckles against the door. We wait. She knocks again, louder. Nothing.

Tamara wraps her hand around the doorknob.

I squeeze my eyes shut in case we're about to commit a heinous violation of Maria's privacy.

"You can open your eyes," Tamara says, her hand still gripping the doorknob. "There's no cereal or underwear."

I open one eye and sneak a tentative peek before committing to open both eyes.

"Which door is Maria's?" I ask, looking down the long hallway lined on both sides with doors.

"There's only one way to find out."

Tamara opens the door enough to step through.

I follow her, and she leaves the door open a crack behind us.

The door on my left says, *Janitorial*. The door on my right says, *Supplies*. Next, we have *Electrical*, then a vague, *Employees Only*.

A rattling doorknob freaks us out. Tamara and I reach for each other and squeeze hands in silent yet dramatic mutual panic. It's like a scene from a 1920s silent movie where the characters can't speak so they overemote and over-gesture to get their point across.

A door at the end of the hall opens, and Twyla steps into the hall. She's wearing the police uniform that got soaked during last night's storm, and her dark hair is in a tight, low bun like it was when we met. Twyla's back is to us. Her left shoulder and hip rest against the doorframe. I can't see Maria, but I hear her voice, so I assume she is standing in front of Twyla or inside the apartment. Twyla's head moves forward. Hands—that I assume belong to Maria—wrap around her khaki uniform shirt. Maria rubs Twyla's back from her shirt collar to the waistband of her khaki police pants and back again, in a lazy up-and-down motion. Smooching noises and occasional giggles pierce the silent hallway.

I suspect we just discovered the real reason for Twyla's visit to the spa last night: Maria.

This is worse than walking in on Maria watching TV and eating cereal in her underwear. We aren't just invading one person's privacy, we're invading two.

We're intruding on an intimate moment we weren't meant to witness.

Should I cough and alert them to our presence? We can pretend we're lost and don't know how we ended up in this off-limits hall. Should Tamara and I try to sneak out the way we snuck in? We must do something. We can't stand here in silence while Maria and Twyla canoodle, oblivious to our presence.

Wide-eyed and engulfed in silent hysteria, Tamara and I tip toe backwards toward Maria's office. I reach behind my back and find the doorknob.

"That was close," Tamara whispers after we escape into Maria's office. "Did you know Maria and Twyla were a couple?"

"No," I whisper in reply. "But I noticed they were familiar with each other last night. They called each other *Mare* and *Twy*."

We press our ears to the door that separates the lobby from Maria's office. Silence. If we're lucky, the front desk is still unattended, and we can sneak away without explaining ourselves.

The clomping of approaching boots alerts us to Twyla's imminent arrival. In a rush to exit Maria's office before Twyla enters it, Tamara opens the door at the exact moment Twyla opens the door on the opposite wall.

I grab Tamara's arm and spin her around so we're facing inside the office as if, by coincidence, we're arriving at the same time as Twyla, not sneaking out before she catches us.

"Perfect timing," I say, smiling and pretending I'm just as surprised to see Twyla as she is to see us.

"Is everything OK, ladies?" Twyla asks, pinching her eyebrows together.

"Fine," I say, smiling.

"Are you looking for Maria?"

"We're looking for you," I reply. "Someone told us you were with Maria."

"Here I am," she says, resting her hands on her slender hips. "You found me."

Twyla gives Tamara and me a head-to-toe scan, and Tamara takes the wad of paper towels from me.

"What's that?" Twyla asks, nodding to the paper towels pressed against Tamara's chest.

"I believe it's spotted water hemlock," Tamara says. "We wrapped it in paper towels in case there are trace amounts of the toxin on the outside of the bag."

"Show me," Twyla says, gesturing to Maria's desk.

Tamara sets the paper towels on the desk and unwraps them, revealing the small baggie of clippings. Twyla inspects the baggie without touching it. Tamara and I sit in the two visitor chairs in front of Maria's desk, then Tamara explains to Twyla why she believes the baggie contains pieces of spotted water hemlock leaves and roots.

"*Cicuta maculata* is quite common around here. It could have come from anywhere," Twyla says. "I've seen clusters of it just outside the property line of the spa.

I assume *Cicuta maculata* is the proper name for

spotted water hemlock. I make a mental note to research spotted water hemlock as soon as I have access to either the internet or cell service.

Using two paper towels to protect her hands, Twyla opens the baggie close to her face and inhales twice, flaring her nostrils.

"Carrots?" Tamara asks.

Twyla nods as she seals the baggie and examines the contents, narrowing her brown eyes as she focuses on specific leaves and clippings.

"I think you're right," Twyla confirms. "It smells and looks like spotted water hemlock." She looks at us. "You found this on a lounge chair?" We nod. "On the deck?" We nod again.

"I suspect there was *cicut*—spotted water hemlock in Summer's Green Powerhouse smoothie," I say, abandoning my attempt to refer to the noxious weed by its botanical nomenclature.

"Explain," Twyla says, crossing her arms in front of her chest and narrowing her eyes at me.

I tell Twyla about the dark green flecks mixed in with Summer's spilled smoothie, and how I assumed the flecks were part of the smoothie until Tamara ordered one, and her smoothie didn't have any.

"And the smoothie Hannah had last night didn't have any dark green flecks either," Tamara adds.

"I'll show you." I unlock my phone and hand it to Twyla with the zoomed-in picture of Summer's regurgitated smoothie on the screen.

"You took photos at the crime scene?" Twyla asks, her mouth agape.

"A few," I reply. "But none that would identify Summer."

"You shouldn't have done that," she chides.

"I did it to preserve evidence," I argue. "In case there was a difference of opinion about the scene."

"I forgot"—Twyla rolls her eyes—"you're the crime scene hobbyist." She thrusts my phone toward me. "Being married to a cop doesn't make you a qualified murder investigator."

"I never claimed to be a qualified murder investigator," I retort, swiping my phone from her.

I open my mouth to protest her labelling me a crime scene hobbyist when the door behind her opens, interrupting our conversation.

"Oh!" Maria says, her eyes flitting around the office, taking in the unexpected scene. "Hello, everyone."

"Does the Green Powerhouse smoothie have dark green flecks, Mare?" Twyla asks.

Maria shakes her head, closing the door behind her "No. It's a consistent minty green colour with a smooth texture. Why?" she asks, sitting at her desk. "What's that?" She points to the baggie topped pile of paper towels on her desk.

Ignoring Maria's question, Twyla tells Maria she needs to talk to everyone who had access to the juice bar yesterday. Maria whips out a pen and makes a few notes on the pad in front of her.

Using her cell phone, Twyla takes photos of the

baggie and its suspicious contents. Still smarting from her crime scene hobbyist comment, I resist the urge to offer her—sarcastically—the photos I took of the baggie in the bathroom.

"I need you to show me where you found it," she says to us. We nod in agreement and stand up. "One at a time," Twyla says, pointing at my chair. "You wait here." I sit down. "First, Tamara will show me, and explain the circumstances around the discovery, then Megan can show me."

"In the meantime, I'll make a list of everyone who had access to the juice bar, and make sure they're available to talk to you," Maria says.

Twyla bundles the baggie into its paper towel nest and places it in a filing cabinet drawer next to Maria's desk. Maria locks the drawer, removes the key from the key ring, and gives it to Twyla.

CHAPTER 16

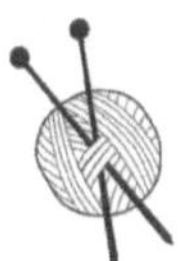

IF I KNEW I would be sitting in Maria's office with nothing to do, I would have kept my knitting instead of asking Hannah to take it back to our room.

"What game are you playing?" Maria asks, nodding at my cell phone.

"I'm not playing a game," I reply. "I'm looking at photos of my husband and dog."

"You have a dog?"

"A corgi," I reply, nodding. "Her name is Sophie."

"Can I see?"

I hand Maria my phone.

"Awww. She's adorable," Maria says. "I wish I could have a dog, but the spa is a pet-free zone. Except for service animals, of course." Her smile is sad and hopeful at the same time. "Is this your husband?"

She turns the phone toward me, and I nod.

"Eric," I say.

"He looks familiar," she says, then scrunches up her mouth. "Have you guys stayed here before?"

"No," I shake my head. "Eric doesn't care for spas, and this is my first visit."

"I'm sure I've seen him somewhere," she says. "Same last name as you?"

I nod. "Sloane."

"Eric Sloane," Maria mutters. "It'll come to me as soon as you leave." She laughs and hands me my phone. "You must miss him and Sophie."

"I do," I admit. "More than I expected. We've only been married four-and-a-half months. Other than a two-day conference he attended last month, this is the longest we've been apart since the wedding. At least when he was at the conference, we could text and talk on the phone."

"It's hard to be away from the love of your life."

Her voice is heavy with experience. I'm tempted to pry but resist.

"Can I ask you a question, Maria?"

"Sure." She looks up from the list she's making. "Shoot."

"Where is Summer?" I ask. "I heard you and Twyla arguing about moving Summer's body to the walk-in fridge." I shift uncomfortably in my seat. "I assume there's only one walk-in fridge, and it's full of food."

"Summer is *not* in the walk-in fridge," Maria insists. "Can you imagine the fallout if Health and Safety found out we stored a corpse with the perishables? Or if the guests found out? I'd lose my job." She guffaws. "I can't justify storing a corpse in the fridge and moving the food somewhere else. Improperly stored food could make people sick." Her eyes widen, and she drops her pen on the desk. "And Nadira would freak out. There's no way she would share her kitchen with a corpse!"

She scoffs, "I told Twy the walk-in fridge is not a morgue, and the topic was closed. She wasn't impressed. She rolled over and turned out her light without even saying goodnight." Panic flashes across her face.

"She's my guest," Maria blurts out the explanation like the words are in a race to leave her mouth. "We're fully booked for Mother's Day," she explains at rapid-fire speed. "I invited Twyla to stay in my apartment." Maria clears her throat. "We're friends."

She fusses with the pencil cup and office supplies on her desk, organizing them by height and making everything face the same direction. "We go way back."

"I figured you were at least friends when I saw you kissing," I confess, not mentioning that Tamara saw it too.

"It's not a secret. It's private," Maria says, looking me in the eye. "Secrecy and privacy aren't the same. I spend all day and night here. It blurs the line between my professional and private life. I just want the same amount of privacy as everyone else."

"It can't be easy when you literally live at work," I sympathize.

"It's not," Maria admits. "I live and work at a remote mountain spa, and Twy lives and works in town. We try to synchronize our days off, but her job is unpredictable, and they call her in on her days off. It's hard on our relationship when we don't spend much time together."

"I get it," I say, my heart stinging with empathy. "My first marriage ended because we didn't prioritize our relationship. The emotional distance made us apathetic, and our connection fizzled."

Maria's eyes well with moisture, and sadness clouds her face. She wipes her eyes with the back of her hand.

"That won't happen to Twy and me." Her voice is light with fake optimism, and an exaggerated smile is plastered across her face. "We have a plan. We're saving for a house." She straightens the piles of paper on her desk. "Somewhere else. Where I can get a job that doesn't require me to live on site. A house with a yard so we can have a dog. Somewhere with a bigger police force where Twy won't be on call twenty-four hours a day, seven days a week."

"I'm rooting for you," I say. "It's not always easy to be with a cop. Especially when you're a person of interest in the case they're investigating."

"I'm not a person of interest in Summer's death." Maria knits her brows together and tilts her head. "Why would you think I'm a person of interest?"

"I heard we're all persons of interest," I reply. "Everyone at the death scene."

"I have an alibi." Maria scoffs and clutches the buttons on her white spa uniform shirt. "I was working the front desk. Remember? You asked me to get a tooth-brush for your mother."

I don't correct her about my connection to Connie, focussing instead on her alibi.

"You disappeared for at least twenty minutes and came back empty-handed," I remind her. "Remember? Your colleague showed up and found the toothbrushes under the counter."

"You don't have an alibi either!" she counters. "You were alone in the lobby when I was searching for a toothbrush."

"We're in the same position," I say. "Our alibis aren't verifiable."

"Twy knows I didn't kill Summer," Maria says, taking off her glasses and cleaning the lenses with the fabric of her shirt. "I gave her a full statement, and I told her who I suspect killed Summer."

"Who?"

"I shouldn't say." She holds up her glasses and inspects the lenses before returning them to her face.

"Is it someone who works at the spa?" I ask, watching to gauge her reaction. She's looks at me like I suggested the Easter Bunny killed Summer. "I'm right, aren't I? You suspect one of your employees murdered Summer."

I do not know if I'm right but hope the suggestion provokes a response from Maria.

"Of course not!" Maria exclaims. "I think it's her sister, Autumn."

"Why?" I ask, shocked by Maria's choice of suspect.

"Two reasons," Maria replies. "First, Twy said murders are almost never random. She said they're almost always committed by someone close to the victim."

She stops talking.

"And?" I urge. "What's the second reason?"

"I heard the twins arguing. More than once. They had issues."

"What did they argue about?"

"Family stuff." Maria shrugs. "This is their first Mother's Day without their mother. Well, for one of them. Summer, was estranged from the family for several years, and their mother died while she was gone. Autumn took care of their mother and buried her. She blamed Summer for their mother's poor health and death. She said their mother's constant worry about Summer lead to her illness. And she resented being their mother's sole caregiver and having to make the final arrangements alone."

"That's unfortunate, but it doesn't mean Autumn killed her sister."

"There's more," Maria says. "Autumn and her mother had a business together. A courier company or something involved with international importing and exporting. When their mother died, Autumn became the sole owner of the business. Summer wanted half of the mother's share, and she wanted Autumn to hire her. Autumn refused."

"Oh," I say, shocked by the conflict and issues

between Autumn and Summer. "How did you overhear this?"

"Spa employees fade into the background," Maria explains. "At first, guests maintain their public personas in our presence, then they stop noticing us, and conduct themselves as though we aren't around."

"Fascinating," I say.

A knock at the door distracts us from our conversation.

"Come in," Maria calls.

"Where's T?" I ask, shifting to peer around Twyla.

"You can see her after I question you. I escorted her to the bistro. She's having lunch with her family. She was eager to make the lunch special. She made me promise to take you there after."

I nod.

"Am I a suspect?" Maria demands, looking at Twyla and drumming her fingers on the desktop.

"Mare, can we talk about this later?"

"So, I am a suspect!"

"That's not what I said."

"It's not what you *didn't* say either."

I sink farther into my chair and hunch my shoulders, hoping not to draw attention to my role as instigator of their domestic dispute.

"Can we discuss this when I'm not conducting interviews?" Twyla opens her palms in a pleading motion.

"Like we discussed the fridge?" Maria challenges, crossing one leg over the other and bouncing her foot in the air. "The kind of discussion where you ignore me, roll over, and go to sleep?"

"I need to use the bathroom," I announce, eager to remove myself from their domestic dispute.

"I'll meet you in the lobby in a few minutes," Twyla says.

"Take your time," I assure her. "I'll be in the massage chair when you're ready."

"I recommend the first setting if you have upper back problems, and the third setting if you have lower back issues." Maria smiles.

CHAPTER 17

"Megan?"

How long have I been here? Five minutes? An hour? Who knows? Time stopped when the massage chair and I became one.

I open one eye just enough to make out my fuzzy surroundings. Twyla stands over me, her feet hip width apart, and her arms crossed in front of her chest. She releases one hand and wiggles her fingers at me when she sees my partially open eye.

"Ready, sleepyhead?" she asks.

I nod and turn off the massage chair.

Outside, I squint into the daylight and lower my sunglasses from the top of my head to my face. Twyla does the same, covering her face with large, mirrored aviators.

"Which chair was it?" she asks.

"Over here." Twyla follows me through the maze of tables and chairs. "Connie and I were walking through here when I heard a sneeze," I say, recounting how we came to occupy the lounge chair.

"And you never saw the baggie before April pulled it out from between the lounge chair cushions?" Twyla asks after I finish telling her the events that preceded her finding Tamara and me in Maria's office with the baggie.

I leave out the part where we witnessed her and Maria sharing an intimate moment outside Maria's apartment.

"None of us had seen it before," I reply. "Connie and I sat here." I point to the lounge chair next to the chair in question. "We never sat in the lounger where April found the baggie."

"It could have fallen between the cushions when Autumn and the doctor bumped into each other," Twyla thinks out loud. "Or it could belong to whoever occupied the lounger before Autumn."

"The killer's fingerprints might be on the plastic baggie," I suggest.

"Your fingerprints might be on the baggie too," Twyla adds. "And April's. And Tamara's."

"Well... yes..." I agree, searching for words to defend myself and my friends. "But we brought the baggie to you. If we killed Summer, why would we hand deliver evidence that implicates us?"

"Sometimes suspects do strange things, Megan," Twyla replies. "You wouldn't be the first perpetrator to deliver the murder weapon to the police and expect to get away with it."

"Murder weapon?" I ask. "Did the killer poison Summer with spotted water hemlock?"

"You said it, not me," Twyla says, raising her hands in surrender.

"I said, I *suspect* the spotted water hemlock *could* be the murder weapon," I clarify. "You said it *is* the murder weapon. And you sounded confident."

"I found Summer and Autumn's smoothie cups in the change room," Twyla admits. "Someone wrapped the cups in paper towels and buried them at the bottom of the garbage can. Would you know anything about that?"

"Of course not!"

"If the killer left their fingerprints on Summer's cup, I'll know who did it. Soon."

"Good!" I declare. "But how will you know which cup belonged to Summer? Don't identical twins have identical fingerprints?"

"No," Twyla replies. "That's a common misconception. Identical twins share DNA, and their fingerprints often appear identical to the naked eye, but under examination, they're not. No two people have the same fingerprints. Even if there are no fingerprints on the cup, only one cup had dark green flecks stuck to the inside."

"The same dark green flecks as the sauna floor and the clippings in the baggie?" I ask.

"It appears so." Twyla nods. "The doctor also found dark green flecks inside Summer's mouth. Listen, Megan, no one can know Summer was murdered, or the murderer laced her smoothie with poisonous leaves."

"They won't find out from us," I say, speaking for all six of us. "By doing the right thing, and handing in the evidence we found, I've made myself a stronger suspect, haven't I?"

"I can't eliminate you," Twyla says. "You don't have an alibi."

"I don't have a *verifiable* alibi," I correct her. "But neither does Maria. Or you.

"Me?!" Twyla scoffs. "Are you serious? You think *I* killed Summer? I'm a law enforcement officer. I uphold the law. I don't break it."

"But you don't have an alibi," I remind her. "You were gone for over twenty minutes to retrieve the satellite phone from your car. It took you twenty minutes to realize your car and the phone were missing?"

"No, it took five minutes to realize the storm washed away my patrol car with the road," Twyla explains. "When I saw the river of mud where the road used to be, I conducted a perimeter check, assessing for potential danger and imminent threats to the spa." She gestures around us. "The perimeter check took longer than expected because of the strong winds and torrential rain."

"Did you check the deck when you checked the perimeter?"

"Of course. That's what perimeter check means, Megan. The entire perimeter."

I hate how often Twyla says my name and the condescending tone with which she says it.

"So, you were right here"—I point to the deck beneath our feet—"around the time Summer died?"

"It's possible." Twyla shrugs. "I'd need the coroner to estimate Summer's time of death to know for sure. Why?"

I point to the door that says *Sauna*.

"You admit you were at the crime scene at the approximate time of Summer's death," I conclude.

"Give me a break. Why would I kill Summer?"

"Why would I?" I counter. "Summer and I met for the first time a few hours before she died. What possible motive could I have to kill her?"

"I don't know," Twyla says, "but if you have one, I'll uncover it."

"How could I have sneaked the spotted water hemlock into Summer's smoothie?"

"You and your daughter were in the change room with Autumn and Summer. You had access to their smoothies."

I hadn't thought of that.

"Twyla, if I killed Summer, why would I return to the scene of the crime to tell you about our encounter with the twins and their smoothies? Then bring you the baggie of poisonous leaves that killed her?"

"Like I said, some perpetrators insert themselves into the investigation so they can keep tabs on it."

"I wouldn't do that," I say, then something Twyla said hits me. "Wait. You said *Hannah and I* had access to

Summer's smoothie in the change room. Is my daughter a suspect?"

"Like I said, Megan. Everyone is a sus—"

"No way! Uh-uh," I cut her off, shaking my head. "Hannah was upstairs with Connie when Summer died. My daughter is not a suspect."

"It's doesn't matter where she was when Summer died," Twyla explains. "If the killer poisoned Summer's smoothie, they did it before she died."

Hannah's status as murder suspect further fuels my determination to uncover the killer.

"What about Nadira?" I ask, searching for compelling suspects besides Hannah. "Autumn and Nadira had multiple confrontations. The smoothie bar is beside her kitchen."

"I'm aware of Autumn's history with Nadira, and I'm investigating all leads."

"And Billie?" I ask, making sure Twyla is aware there is an entire spa filled with suspects besides my daughter. "She's close to the twins. She had access to Summer. They shared a room for goodness' sake. Where was Billie between the blackout and when she showed up at the bistro? She showed up late, more than halfway through Maria's speech. Also, she hasn't stopped puking since we found Summer's body. Could the guilt of killing one of her best friends be making her sick? Or maybe her nausea is a symptom because she had contact with the spotted water hemlock when she cut it up and added it to Summer's smoothie."

"That's not how spotted water hemlock works,

Megan," Twyla explains. "Summer's death would have been painful, violent, and fast. Chronic nausea isn't a symptom."

"My point is," I clarify, "there are plenty of suspects with motives and unverified alibis who actually *knew* Summer. Hannah and I only met her yesterday."

"I get your point, Megan. You're trying to prove how observant you are. But like I said, if the killer poisoned her, they didn't have to be anywhere near Summer when she died."

"But they returned to the scene of the crime to pose her body," I argue. "Summer didn't drop dead behind the pentagon bench with her legs bent and her body tucked conveniently out of sight."

"I'm investigating every possible angle and every possible suspect," Twyla reiterates. "I'm retracing Summer's last hours and talking to everyone who had access to her or her smoothie prior to her death."

"Have you considered that Summer's killer might be someone from her past?" I ask, refusing to stop listing alternate suspects. "Summer's murder could have been a professional hit."

"What are you talking about?" Twyla asks, chuckling and dismissing my suggestion with a shake of her head.

"Are you aware that Summer was in witness protection?" I demand. "According to her sister, Summer witnessed a murder and her testimony helped convict a mob boss's son. Her testimony put her life in danger. Serious danger. Danger that made her give up her family, her life, and her identity. Summer's killer could have been exacting revenge."

"Shhh!" Twyla takes my upper arm and leads me off the deck to a secluded corner of the garden. "Autumn told you this?" she hisses. "What else did Autumn tell you?"

"Not much," I reply. "She said Summer's testimony and life in witness protection was a selfless act of courage, and they lost ten years together that they'll never get back. She wasn't gossiping, she was trying to portray what kind of person Summer was."

"This isn't public knowledge," Twyla whispers. "I'm shocked Autumn mentioned it to you."

"You already knew," I allege. "You're not surprised by Summer's past, you're surprised I *know* about it."

"Of course, I already knew," Twyla snaps.

"Is that the real reason you drove to the spa in such dangerous weather? Were you assigned to check on her?"

"Something like that," Twyla says, grinding her jaw and fixating on a random daffodil. "Who else knows about Summer's past? Who was there when Autumn told you?"

"Connie," I reply.

"Megan, you're in over your head. You have no idea what you're talking about, and I won't allow you to compromise this case." Twyla removes her sunglasses and locks eyes with me. She takes a single step forward. A step that, combined with her fierce, unblinking glare, intimidates me. Is that her intention? Is Twyla threatening me? "Do not interfere in this investigation, Megan," she warns. "Do you understand? Being an investigator's wife doesn't qualify you to solve a murder."

I swallow hard and defy my body's instinct to step back in retreat. Aware that my body is leaning away from her, and refusing to let Twyla see she intimidates me, I pull myself up to my full five feet, two-and-three-quarter inches and take a half step forward, meeting her gaze. "Actually, I'm a police chief's wife," I correct her, overemphasizing my *f's*. "And you should get used to me asking questions because if solving this murder is the only way to eliminate Hannah and me as suspects, I intend to find Summer's killer."

CHAPTER 18

WE FINISH INTERROGATING EACH OTHER, and Twyla escorts me to the bistro.

"Where are Hannah and Rachel?" I ask, joining them at the table.

"They went to the eyebrow and lash bar," Connie replies.

"Then they're having an effleurage scalp massage with aromatherapy," Tamara adds.

"Was the Zucchini Roshti Yucca Burger with French Mustard Dressing yummy?" I ask, gesturing to the empty plate in front of Tamara.

"Very," she replies, smiling and rubbing circles on her tummy.

"I guess I'm too late to order it." I check the time on my cell phone, and the lunch special ended ten minutes ago.

"We've got your back, Megabyte." April nods, looking behind me.

Nadira approaches our table, smiling and carrying a tray.

"Your friends asked me to save you a plate," she says, setting the dish in front of me.

"Thank you," I say, smiling up at her, then turning to my three friends. "And thank you. I'm starving."

"Thanks for breaking the rule and serving this outside of the two-hour window," Tamara says.

"It's my rule," Nadira says. "If I can't break it, who can?" She chuckles.

"Join us, Chef," Tamara insists.

"I shouldn't." Nadira scans the almost-empty room.

"C'mon," April urges. "The lunch rush is over. Take a break."

"OK, but just for a moment," Nadira says, pulling out the chair between me and Connie.

While I savour Nadira's vegan masterpiece, we make small talk and pepper the chef with compliments on her gastronomic genius.

April and Tamara excuse themselves to attend an appointment for lymphatic drainage massage, which somehow sounds relaxing and unappealing at the same time.

Nadira, Connie, and I are alone in the bistro dining room.

I nod, pretending to listen to Connie and Nadira's friendly chitchat, while brainstorming how to bring up Summer's death without bringing down Nadira's relaxed, chatty mood. This could be my only opportunity to ask her about her and Autumn's confrontational history. Next thing I know, Connie steers the conversation for me.

"Megan and I ran into Autumn earlier," Connie says, changing the subject like some kind of mind-reading fairy godmother. "She seems to still be in shock. Poor thing. I hope she's eating. She needs to keep up her strength. With Billie's tummy trouble, I doubt she'll make sure Autumn eats enough and stays hydrated. Have you seen Autumn? Did she come downstairs for breakfast or lunch?"

Well done, Connie! I'm tempted to give her a standing ovation but settle for turning my full attention to Nadira, awaiting her response.

"We've delivered Autumn's meals to her room," Nadira replies. "Her dishes came back to the kitchen with less food than when we delivered them." She shrugs one shoulder. "I assume she's eating."

"That's good." Connie smiles sadly.

"Did Autumn say anything else when you ran into her?" Nadira asks. "Anything about me?"

Connie nods, looking at me to chime in.

"She said the chicken you served her triggered the migraine symptoms that caused her to leave Summer alone before she died."

Nadira huffs, accompanied by a head shake and eye roll.

"She didn't even eat the chicken," Nadira argues. "How could it have triggered a migraine?"

Connie and I look at each other, then at Nadira.

"I know you said confusing the chicken with the

tofu was an honest mistake, but Autumn insists you did it on purpose."

"Why?" Nadira demands. "What satisfaction would I get from feeding chicken to a pescatarian? Why would I provoke another verbal attack from Autumn?"

"Yes," Connie sympathizes. "Billie told us about Autumn's aggressive form of advocating."

"I don't know why Billie is nauseous all the time," Nadira defends. "And I know she and Autumn claim the nausea started when she came to the spa and started eating food I'd prepared, but I assure you, it's not my cooking. Contrary to what Autumn claims, I don't use secret ingredients. I disclose every ingredient in every dish. Whatever is wrong with Billie has nothing to do with me."

"Yesterday, I tried to order tofu," I say, "but the server told me the spa hasn't had tofu all week."

"It's true," Nadira admits. "Our tofu order wasn't on the delivery truck. I told the staff to tell guests that tofu is off the menu. But there is a small amount left in the kitchen. I put it aside for guests who have special dietary needs or allergies."

"So, you rationed the remaining tofu?" I clarify.

"Yes."

"And you intended to use some of it in Autumn's order yesterday?"

"Yes," Nadira replies. "I wanted to avoid another confrontation with her. If I didn't accommodate Autumn's tofu request, she would have made a big deal about it. I got distracted. The cubed chicken and cubed tofu were next to each other in identical bowls. I picked up the cubed chicken instead of the tofu by accident." She brings her hand to the top button of her chef's jacket. "It was an honest mistake. I would never intentionally contaminate food. No matter how much I dislike the guest who ordered it."

She admits she doesn't like Autumn, and she knows Autumn is spreading rumours about undisclosed ingredients and Nadira's food causing Billie's stomach issues.

"Has Autumn confronted you about anything since Summer died?"

"No," Nadira replies. "I haven't seen Autumn since dinner last night. Except for when she ran in here searching for Summer."

"It must infuriate you that Autumn questioned your professional integrity," Connie comments.

"I was infuriated at first," Nadira admits. "Then I realized this is how Autumn is. Arguing encourages her. So, I stopped arguing. When she would yell and try to goad me into an altercation, I nodded until she finished, then I thanked her for her feedback and walked away. But yesterday morning she threatened to make it a bigger issue. She threatened to contact food bloggers and leave negative reviews at restaurants where I've worked."

"How did you react when she threatened your livelihood?" I ask.

"I counter-threatened her," Nadira admits. Connie lets out a small gasp, and Nadira turns to her. "With my lawyer," she clarifies. "I threatened to sue her for slander. Or libel. Or whatever they call it when someone spreads lies to ruin a person's reputation."

"I bet Autumn didn't like that," I say.

"Not at all," Nadira confirms. "She said it wasn't slander because it was true." She raises her hands in a conciliatory gesture and looks back and forth between Connie and me. "It's not. None of Autumn's accusations against me are true."

We stop talking when the server removes the last of the dirty dishes and offers to refill our drinks.

After watching the server walk toward the kitchen with an armful of plates and cutlery, Nadira leans toward me.

"Did Autumn tell you I killed Summer?" she asks.

"Why would you ask that?" I ask.

"The questions Twyla asked me earlier made me think Autumn accused me of killing her sister."

"She told us she thinks you did it," Connie admits.

"Why would I kill Summer? I had barely said two words to her since they checked in."

"Autumn believes she was the intended victim," I explain. "She thinks you planned to kill her to stop her from ruining your career, but you accidentally killed the wrong twin."

"I didn't kill anyone," Nadira insists. "Autumn should look closer to home if she wants to find her sister's killer."

"What does that mean?" I ask, squishing my brows toward each other.

"It means, why isn't Billie a suspect?" Nadira asks. "I overheard Billie and Autumn talking one day when they were eating alone. Billie warned Autumn not to trust Summer. If I recall, her exact words were, *I know she's your sister, but you know what Summer is like. Don't trust her too much, too soon.* Then Billie warned Autumn that *Summer might be up to her old tricks,* whatever that means."

"How did Autumn respond?" I ask. "Did she defend her sister?"

"Autumn told Billie not to worry because, in her words, *I know Summer better than anyone and can tell when she's lying.* Then Autumn told Billie she would *be careful and let Summer in slowly.*"

"Let Summer into what slowly?" Connie asks.

"I don't know," Nadira replies. "I only heard a snippet of their conversation."

Were Autumn and Billie talking about letting Summer into the family business? According to Maria, Summer wanted Autumn to hire her and give her half of their mother's share. Or maybe Autumn meant she would let Summer into her heart slowly? After years of no contact, the sisters could have had some issues to work through. I need to speak to Billie and Autumn again and find out the context of the conversation Nadira overheard.

"Who worked at the juice bar last night after dinner?" I ask, trying to figure out who else I should add to my to-be-questioned list.

"Me," Nadira replies. "I filled in as a last-minute favour for Maria."

"Why would a world-renowned chef fill in at a juice bar?" I ask.

"Maria was desperate," Nadira replies. "I was in the middle of today's meal prep, but she begged me. She covered the juice bar until I finished cleaning the kitchen and took over. She said she double-booked the staff member who was scheduled to work. She said the schedule was a mess. I agreed to fill in for thirty minutes while Maria sorted out the schedule and found someone to take over for me. But I ended up working there until the blackout."

"That means you made Hannah's smoothie last night," Connie concludes, clapping her hands once in front of her chest. "I had a sip. It was delicious." She smiles and crinkles her nose.

"Thank you," Nadira says. "Yes, I made Hannah's Green Powerhouse smoothie, but I can't take credit. I didn't create the smoothie menu, they established it before I started working here."

"Did you make Autumn and Summer's smoothies too?" I ask, intentionally not mentioning the specific smoothies they ordered.

Nadira shakes her head. "Billie visited the smoothie bar. I don't remember the exact time, but she was there before Hannah."

"What did Billie order?" I ask.

"Three Green Powerhouse smoothies," Nadira

replies. "It's by far the most popular item on the smoothie menu."

"Did Billie customize any of the smoothies?" I ask, in case she requested an additional dark green, leafy ingredient.

"Nope. She just ordered three Green Powerhouse smoothies."

"Was Billie alone?" I ask.

"She approached the juice bar alone," Nadira replies. "But a twin was waiting for her several feet away."

"Which twin?" I ask.

"Beats me," Nadira admits, shrugging. "I can't tell them apart. I spend most of my time in the kitchen. I have very little interaction with guests. Except Autumn. I've had more than enough interaction with Autumn."

CHAPTER 19

"How did you get in?" I ask. "It's the most popular treatment at the resort. Hot Stone massages are booked months in advance."

Earlier, when Connie and I spoke with Autumn, I made a flippant remark about getting a hot stone massage. Connie picked up on it, cancelled the afternoon treatments we had already booked, and scheduled hot-stone massages instead.

"I can be persuasive when the situation warrants it," Connie replies, her chin held high. "Also, the receptionist said they've had a few cancellations today. Apparently, some guests have lost their appetite for spa treatments since Summer's death."

With time to kill until our massages, we take a stroll through the gardens and enjoy the warm, spring air. Like most people who live with long, cold winters, we don't take spring for granted. We use any excuse to soak up the sunshine and mild temperatures.

"What's your opinion of Nadira, my dear?" Connie asks, as we wander through the herb garden, stopping to read the small information placards about each sprouting herb.

"She's a talented chef," I reply.

"That's not what I mean"—Connie swats my arm playfully—"Do you think she killed Summer?"

"We can't rule her out," I say. "She admits she didn't like Autumn, and she admits Autumn threatened to slander her and ruin her career. That's motive. She also admits she couldn't tell Summer and Autumn apart. Autumn could be right about Summer's murder being a case of mistaken identity."

"And let's not forget, Nadira had access to the smoothie ingredients," Connie reminds me.

"But if she made three identical smoothies, how could she ensure her intended victim would get the poisoned one?" I ask. "Unless Billie told her two of the smoothies were for the twins, how could Nadira have known two smoothies were for Autumn and Summer?"

"Maybe Nadira and Billie were in on it together," Connie suggests.

"If Billie and Nadira worked together to kill Summer, that would imply they knew each other before Billie and the twins checked into the spa," I surmise.

"Committing murder together is a commitment," Connie advises. "Murder is a big secret to trust with someone you don't know well."

We stop while Connie photographs the tulips.

"Maria had access to the smoothie ingredients too,"

I say. "She worked at the smoothie bar until Nadira relieved her."

"Maybe Maria murdered Summer and planted the chef at the smoothie bar to implicate Nadira as the killer."

"What motive would Maria have?" I ask. "Why would she want Summer dead?"

"Not Summer, my dear, Autumn," Connie clarifies. "If Autumn follows through on her threat to slander Nadira and leave negative reviews online, those reviews and accusations would stain the spa's reputation too."

"You're right," I agree. "Earlier, Maria mentioned that she's saving to buy a house. She wants to move and find a job that doesn't require her to live on site. Bad reviews, accusations about contaminated food, and sick guests wouldn't look good on her resume," I speculate.

If Maria killed Summer, would Twyla help her cover up the crime? Love is a powerful motive, and from what I witnessed outside Maria's apartment this morning, Twyla and Maria love each other. Twyla is in the perfect position to manipulate the investigation. She could point the evidence away from Maria or even destroy evidence that implicates her.

She's the only law enforcement officer here. Twyla oversees the collection and preservation of all the evidence. What if, when Tamara and I gave the baggie of spotted water hemlock to Twyla, we pointed the finger of suspicion at Maria, foiling Twyla's plan to pin Summer's murder on someone else? What if Maria's fingerprints are on the baggie? This would explain Twyla's intimidation tactic when she warned me to stop asking questions. She was protecting Maria.

Or was Twyla protecting herself?

Did Twyla kill Summer? Is she a crooked cop? Does she work for the family of the man Summer testified against? Autumn said the man who Summer testified against, and his father, are dead, so their vendetta against Summer died with them. But what if that's not true? What if other family members kept the grudge alive? Biding their time, patiently and quietly waiting for Summer to reveal herself by resuming her old life and identity so they could kill her.

Maybe Maria helped Twyla by giving her access to the spa. I wonder if Maria is aware of Summer's history with the police and the witness protection program? Twyla admitted she knew about Summer's past. Maybe she confided in Maria. Goodness knows, Eric confides in me and discloses things we both know he shouldn't. Twyla and Maria could have a similar dynamic.

"We should make our way inside," Connie says, distracting me from my thoughts. "If we start now, we'll be fashionably punctual for our massage appointments."

We circle the cluster of yet-to-bloom rose bushes in the centre of the garden that act as a roundabout, and veer toward the main building. As we meander past the hummingbird garden, I can't stop thinking about Twyla's coincidental arrival at the spa just before Summer died. She said she was checking on the spa because of the storm, but her trip to SoulSpring Spa and Retreat is suspicious. Her arrival coincided with a murder, and she made the drive in treacherous conditions. Twyla has no verifiable alibi. She's unaccounted for from just before the blackout until after the generators kicked in.

Maria was also unaccounted for much of that time. Was that a coincidence, or part of their premeditated plan? Maria knew Summer was in the sauna. She has access to the appointments for each spa treatment, and because Autumn visited the front desk to ask for pain medication, Maria knew Summer was alone.

Why did Twyla really come to the spa last night? Did her boss dispatch her to check on the remote location? After finding out about Twyla and Maria's personal relationship, I assumed the real reason for Twyla's visit on a dark and stormy night was to make sure Maria was safe. But maybe Twyla's motivation was neither direct orders, nor her love for Maria. Maybe she came here to kill Summer, and the power failure and storm damage were unplanned coincidences. I'm lost in my own thoughts, contemplating whether Maria and Twyla acted together or if one of them killed Summer alone, when Connie hooks her arm through mine and speaks.

"I have one more surprise for you, my dear," she teases. "I arranged for you to have the same massage therapist as Billie."

"You did?" I ask, wide-eyed. "Maybe I can confirm Billie's story about leaving with the massage therapist when the power went out. Wherever she went after the power failure, it wasn't the Epicurean Bistro."

"Billie's grief and shock about Summer's death seem genuine," Connie observes. "But it can't be easy being best friends with twin sisters. Billie must have felt left out sometimes. Summer left for a decade, and Billie was used to having Autumn to herself."

"I've had the same thought," I confess. "I'm sure at least a small part of Billie was jealous when Summer returned. I'd also like to know more about the snippet of conversation Nadira overheard between Billie and Autumn. Did Billie warn Autumn to be careful trusting her sister because she had a reason to question Summer's intentions, or was she jealous of Autumn and Summer's reconnection?"

"I don't know," Connie replies. "But if we noticed Billie's late arrival, Twyla noticed, too, and has already asked her about it." We slow our already leisurely pace and lower our voices as we get closer to the massage area. "Billie had access to the smoothies," Connie points out. "In fact, one could argue Billie *controlled* the smoothies. She ordered them, carried them away from the juice bar, and she could have chosen which smoothie to give to each twin."

"But if Nadira was at the Smoothie bar, and one twin was a few feet away, Billie couldn't have poisoned the smoothie without Nadira or the twin seeing her."

"What if the twin waiting near the smoothie bar was Autumn?" Connie suggests. "What if Autumn and Billie went to the smoothie bar together?"

"Why would Autumn and Billie conspire to kill Summer?"

"We already know Billie's motive, my dear. Jealousy. Maybe Billie convinced Autumn to help."

"Autumn doesn't strike me as someone who would be easy to manipulate," I reply. "If you'd seen her shouting at Nadira yesterday, you'd know what I mean. But you could be on to something. When the twins' mother died, Autumn became the sole owner of the family business. Summer wanted Autumn to hire her and give her half of their mother's shares."

"Maybe Autumn didn't want to share," Connie suggests.

"They also argued about their mother. Autumn blamed Summer for their mother's declining health and eventual death. She said the stress of Summer's testimony and losing contact when she went into witness protection, triggered the decline in her health and, ultimately, her death. Autumn also resented being their mother's sole caregiver."

"Did Autumn and Summer resolve these issues before Summer died?" Connie asks.

"I don't know," I reply.

"If Autumn is innocent of her sister's murder, the weight of her mother's death and her sister's murder are heavy enough without the added burden of unresolved issues."

"I know," I agree. "My heart breaks for Autumn and everything she's endured."

"But?" Connie asks. "I sense a *but*."

"But something Autumn did last night still bothers me." We stop outside the door. "Why did she visit the front desk for pain medication?" I ask in a whisper. "She suffers with chronic migraines and carries prescription medication with her. She even brought it to the deck today. She said the prescription medication is a last resort because of the side effects. If that's true, why does she carry the prescription medication but not ibuprofen, or acetaminophen, or whatever? It doesn't make sense."

"Why did I pack two tubes of toothpaste and forget my toothbrush?" Connie asks. "Whatever the reason, it sounds like you still have more questions than answers, my dear."

I intend to find the answers.

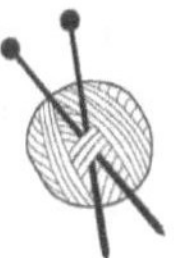

CHAPTER 20

I sit on the massage table in the centre of the dimly lit room and smooth the white cotton sheets around me. I'm sure this is ambient lighting and not an energy-saving tactic. Shelves of folded, white linens line one wall, and shelves displaying crystals, self-care books, and other accessories that promote relaxation line another. The third wall features a sink and cabinet with a hotel landline phone. The emergency exit takes up most of the fourth wall. Soft guitar music plays from strategically mounted speakers that someone painted to camouflage with the walls. A familiar guitar chord catches my ear. It's from the chorus of a popular song, rearranged and slowed down. I hum along to the familiar tune, trying to place it. The exact moment the song title and artist pops into my head—*In My Life* by The Beatles—the massage room door opens and a smiley, short-haired, petite young woman in wire-framed, round glasses greets me.

"Namaste." She brings her hands together under her chin, averting her gaze downward for an instant.

"Namaste," I return, giving a slight nod, but skipping the prayer hands.

The massage therapist's name tag reads, *Logan S.*

On tippy toes, Logan reaches for the top shelf and feels around. When she lowers her heels to the floor, she's holding a red barbecue lighter and a box of incense. She slides an incense stick from the box, positions it in the wooden incense burner, and ignites it. Logan blows out the flame, leaving a tiny orange ember tip. A thin line of smoke dances toward the ceiling.

"We have the same last name," Logan informs me pointing to her name tag. "Except I spell it S-L-O-N-E."

"We were one letter away from running into each other at a family reunion," I joke.

Logan discovers more similarities. Besides our surnames being homonyms, our first names are two syllables, five letters, have a hard *g* in the middle, and end with *an*. The similarities intrigue the massage therapist, and she wonders out loud if there could be a universal significance. As Logan ruminates over the coincidences of our names, searching for a deeper meaning behind us meeting and a message from the universe, I hope the bond we've forged over our similar names increases the likelihood that Logan will be comfortable talking to me about Billie's massage last night.

The aroma from the incense stick hits my nose.

"Citrus?" I ask, inhaling and changing the subject.

"Yes," Logan replies, returning the incense and lighter to the top shelf. "It's a blend of frankincense, orange, and vetiver. This combination of aromas promotes relaxation and relieves stress. If you like it, you can buy it in the gift shop near the main entrance." Panic flashes across her face. "Is it OK?" she blurts, her eyes bulging. "I should've asked first. I'm sorry."

Logan motions to extinguish the incense stick.

"No," I say, stopping her before she covers the burning ember. "It's fine. It's a lovely scent."

"Are you sure?" she confirms.

"Positive." I smile. "Don't worry. If I didn't like it, I would tell you."

Logan sucks in a deep breath and lets it out slowly.

"Last night a client reacted to the incense," Logan admits. "I think it made her sick, but she was too polite to admit it. She turned a weird shade of green and broke out in a sweat."

Though not a description of her appearance, Logan's description of her client's nausea matches Billie to a tee.

"I think that was my friend, Billie," I say, exaggerating our relationship status.

"Right," Logan confirms. "It was Billie. Is she feeling better today?"

"She's fine," I assure the worried massage therapist. "I don't think the incense caused Billie's nausea. She's had a tummy bug for a couple of days."

"Well, regardless," Logan announces. "I learned a valuable lesson. I shouldn't introduce aromas without asking first."

Logan asks me a series of health questions, then explains how the hot stone massage will work. I fill out a brief questionnaire, sign a liability waiver, then Logan leaves the room while I undress.

"Come in," I say when she taps on the door.

"Ready?" she asks.

"Ready," I reply.

While Logan washes her hands, I shift one last time, ensuring I'm comfy, and hope I don't get a hard-to-ignore itchy nose partway through the massage.

"So, what made you decide to book a hot stone massage?" Logan asks, placing a small, warm stone between my eyebrows.

"My friend, Billie, suggested it," I reply, moving my mouth as little as possible as Logan places a small stone on each of my cheeks.

"Hmmm," Logan mutters, balancing a small stone on my chin. "I'm surprised she had such a positive experience. The power went out right after I started her massage. I had to stop."

"She told me," I mumble, trying to not disturb the stones.

"I feel terrible about that," Logan says. "First her massage started late, then it ended early."

"Started late?" I mumble, trying to make eye contact with Logan without moving my head.

"Palms up," Logan says, ignoring my question.

I turn my palms toward the sky.

"Why did Billie's massage start late?" I ask again, hoping that Logan's experience administering hot stone massages has helped her to develop the dentist-like ability to understand the mumbles of people who can't move their mouth.

"It was partly my fault, and partly Billie's," Logan explains, pressing a warm stone onto each of my palms. "When I left the room while Billie undressed, I found my friend crying in the hall."

"Oh, no!" I respond. "Why?"

"She had a huge fight with her boyfriend on the phone. She accused him of cheating. They almost broke up! I consoled my friend and left Billie longer than I should. When my friend's cell phone rang—it was her boyfriend—I excused myself to check on Billie, but she wasn't here."

"What?" I open my mouth too wide, and the stone on my chin slides onto the massage table beside my head. "Where was she?"

"Careful," Logan says replacing the fallen stone. "I don't know where she went. I knocked, but Billie didn't answer. I opened the door to check on her, and she was gone. She must have left through the back door"— Logan points to the emergency exit—"because my friend and I were in the hall, and there's no way Billie could have slipped past without us noticing."

"Wouldn't an alarm go off if Billie left through the emergency exit?"

"No," Logan replies. "The emergency exits don't have alarms, and they're only locked at night. Employees use them all the time to get from one part of the spa to another. It's quicker than navigating through the building."

"What did you do when Billie disappeared?"

"I went back to my friend in the hall," Logan replies, placing a warm stone on my right collarbone. "She was still talking to her boyfriend, and their conversation was kind of loud. I had to ask her to keep it down."

She places a warm stone on my left collarbone.

"Then what?"

"My friend went back to the sauna reception desk, and I knocked on Billie's door again."

Excuse me?! Logan's friend left the reception desk in the spa area? This explains why the sauna attendant didn't see the killer return to the sauna to pose Summer's body.

"Your friend worked at the sauna reception desk last night?" I confirm as Logan lays two larger, warm stones along my breast bone.

"Yup." Logan nods. "Where that guest turned up dead. She never saw the body though."

I gasp, but get it under control when the stones on my face wiggle. Luckily, they don't fall.

"How is your friend doing today?" I ask.

"She's OK," Logan replies, using a large, warm, oily stone to massage my arm. "It was a misunderstanding. She made up with her boyfriend before we lost cell service and the power went out."

I wasn't asking about her friend's love life. I'm curious how Logan's friend is holding up after having a guest die in the sauna during her shift. But I'm also kind of curious about the boyfriend situation, so I probe further.

"What kind of misunderstanding?"

"A guest told my friend that a massage therapist was bragging about stealing my friend's boyfriend. My friend asked the guest which therapist, but the guest didn't know her name. She gave my friend a vague description and told her she could catch them together in a massage therapy room, at that moment."

"Did she catch them?"

"Nope. The massage rooms were full of guests having legitimate massages. When she didn't find him, she called him on her cell phone. They were arguing when the call was dropped because cell service was unreliable during the storm. That's when I found her in the hall."

"Your friend must've been away from the sauna for quite a while," I surmise.

"I guess," Logan says, rubbing an oil-infused hot stone into my leg muscles.

"Which guest told your friend her boyfriend was cheating?"

"An anonymous guest," Logan replies. "The woman called from an internal line. She didn't give her name, and the landline went down before my friend could ask anything."

Did the landline cut out, or did the guest hang up before the sauna attendant figured out their identity? If I was a betting woman, I bet the killer called the sauna attendant with a made-up story to lure her away from her post. Then the killer returned to the sauna, confirmed Summer was dead, and positioned her body to delay the discovery.

But how did the killer know what would enrage her enough to leave her post? How did the killer know about the attendant's boyfriend? Or that she would believe he was cheating?

Billie could've used the landline in this room to call the sauna, convince the attendant to abandon her post, then use the emergency exits to sneak to the sauna area and sneak back again before Logan returned. Nerves could have caused the nausea that Logan witnessed. If Billie was about to commit murder, she was bound to be anxious and sick to her stomach.

"Did you and Billie leave together after the power went out?" I ask.

"Yup. We were the last two people here," Logan replies. "I was the key holder last night. It was my job to turn off everything and lock up. I continued Billie's massage as long as possible after the power failure because I felt bad that we had just gotten started. But the stones cool down fast without the heater, and I couldn't see in the dark. We left together, but my friend was waiting for me. I turned to say goodnight to Billie and apologize again for her interrupted massage, but she was gone." Logan shrugs. "Ready to flip over so I can do your back?"

She removes the stones from my body and I turn onto my stomach under the white sheet.

"Besides the many physical benefits, hot stone

massage also has mental health benefits," Logan informs me. "It promotes stress reduction and better sleep quality, which results in improved mental clarity. The benefits will be more obvious to you tomorrow, after a good night's sleep."

"I already feel them," I say. "You've given me more mental clarity than I've had since I checked in."

CHAPTER 21

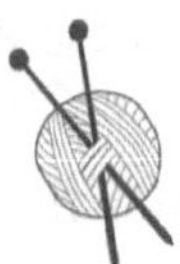

"It sounds like your hot stone massage was very informative," Connie comments.

"Thank you again," I say, thanking her for at least the fifth time since our massages ended. "If you hadn't arranged for Logan to do my massage, we wouldn't know about Billie's disappearing act from the massage room or the coincidental disappearance of the sauna attendant."

"Hey, did you guys hear the helicopter?" April asks, power-walking toward us.

Connie and I halt at the stairwell entrance, shaking our heads.

"There was a helicopter!" Tamara announces, jogging to catch up.

"Did it land?" Connie asks, pushing open the stairwell door.

"No," Tamara replies. "It flew around in circles."

She makes circles in the air with her index finger. "It only hovered for a couple of minutes."

"It was a police helicopter," April says as we climb the first flight of stairs. "Maria said they're checking on the spa and making sure we're OK after last night's storm and power failure and everything.

"Did they drop off a satellite phone?" I ask.

"No one said anything about a satellite phone," April replies. "But at least they know we're stranded, and they're trying to get to us."

"Maria said the helicopter can't land near the spa or fly too low because of the mountains or something," Tamara adds.

We climb the stairs, each of us summarizing and reviewing the spa treatments we received this afternoon. When we reach the third floor, I hold the door while Connie, Tamara, then April file into the hall. We greet the spa employee who's stationed on our floor. She's sitting cross-legged on the floor near the elevator. She picks up a magazine from the pile on the floor next to her and leafs through it.

Connie and Tamara are several paces ahead of April and me when we pass Autumn and Billie's room.

"I'm glad they're eating," Connie comments, looking back at me and pointing to the cart of empty dishes outside Autumn and Billie's room.

I glance at the empty dinner plates on the food cart. One plate is smeared with remnants of a white sauce, and the other plate is empty except for a lamb chop bone picked clean of meat.

"Hopefully those empty dishes are a sign that Autumn is keeping her strength up, and Billie's nausea is improving," Connie observes.

April and Tamara stop at their door, and Connie and I stop at ours. We agree on a time to meet for dinner, then unlock our respective doors and step inside.

"Finally! You're back!" Hannah rushes toward Connie and me with her cell phone in her hand and grips my arm, tugging me forward.

"What's wrong?" I follow my daughter's urgent gaze and find Twyla at the other end. "Why are you here?"

"I wanted to find you, Mum, but I didn't want to leave her here alone. She was already inside the room when Rachel and I got back from having our ears candled." She holds up her phone and scans each of our faces. "I'm recording audio and video footage of everyone and everything in Room 308 at the SoulSpring Spa and Retreat. Today's date is Saturday May, 7th, and the time is 3:27p.m." She points at me and nods, like a director cuing my line.

"Well?" I ask, glaring at Twyla.

"I'm searching for something." She gestures to the open suitcase on the bed next to her.

"In my belongings?" I ask. "Without a warrant?"

Hannah raises her phone and points it at Twyla, waiting for an answer. In my peripheral vision, I see the red dot on Hannah's screen that indicates she's recording.

"I don't need a warrant because I believe this search

is necessary to prevent evidence of a crime from being contaminated, lost, or destroyed."

"What evidence?" Connie asks.

Twyla says nothing.

"You have to tell us what you're searching for," Hannah pipes in. "I study law and my dad is an attorney."

Twyla squints at me. "You told me your husband is a cop."

"Hannah's dad isn't my husband," I explain. "What are you searching for?"

"A key," Twyla says. "The key to sauna three is missing. No one has seen it since last night."

"Why would I have it?"

"According to your statement, the keyring was in your possession last night," Twyla states.

"There were at least a dozen keys on the keyring," I recall. "I tried a few, but they didn't fit. April broke the window with the fire extinguisher and unlocked the door from the inside."

"Where did you put the key ring?" Twyla asks.

"This is in my statement," I remind her. "I tossed it onto the reception desk. I didn't touch it again."

"Did you remove any keys from the keyring?"

"No."

"Did you see April remove any keys from the keyring?"

"No."

"Did you see anyone touch the keyring last night?"

"Yes," I reply. "Maria. Remember? She used the keys

to unlock the sauna where you questioned us. I also saw her trying to fit different keys into the sauna three lock when you taped the broken window. And you had the key ring when you unlocked the door to sauna four."

Twyla's jaw clenches, and the muscles around her eyes tense. My insinuation that her or Maria could have taken the key will probably make Twyla hate me more than she does already, but she asked me a question and I gave her an honest answer. It's not my fault she doesn't like it.

"Anyone else?"

"No," I reply. "The sauna attendant would have used it to lock the door before she left. Did you ask her?"

"She said sauna three was already locked."

"If she didn't lock it, who did?" Hannah asks.

"You know she left her post, right?" I ask. "The sauna attendant visited the massage area because an anonymous caller tipped her off about her boyfriend having a secret tryst in a massage room. She was gone for a while. Long enough for the killer to return to the sauna, stage Summer's body, and steal the key you're looking for."

Twyla blinks. "And?"

Her expression and tone give nothing away. I can't tell if this is new information to Twyla. If the police academy teaches a course on giving the perfect poker face, Twyla aced it.

"Listen, Megan"—Twyla inhales an exasperated

breath and blows it out—"I'm not here to brainstorm potential scenarios with you. We aren't partners. You aren't even an investigator. If you don't have the missing key, consent to the search."

"You're going to search with or without my consent," I cede. "Do whatever you need to do, Twyla, but I'm not letting you out of my sight, and Hannah is recording every move you make."

"This is too much conflict for me," Connie announces. "If anyone needs me, I'll be next door making a cocktail with whatever alcohol I find in April and Tamara's minibar." She slides a strap off her shoulder and opens her tote bag, looking at Twyla. "Would you like to search it before I leave, Officer?"

"No thank you, ma'am." Twyla nods and gives Connie a slight smile. "That won't be necessary."

"Are you searching every guest or just me?" I ask as Twyla inspects the contents of my toiletries bag.

"Everyone who was at the scene last night," she replies, shoving my toiletries back inside the bag, then opening the cabinet under the sink and using her flashlight to search inside.

"How did you find out the sauna was unattended?" Twyla asks as we leave the bathroom. "Were you snooping again?"

Did she just roll her eyes? I make a mental note to check Hannah's footage later to see if the eye roll was real or if I imagined it.

"I found out by coincidence during an unrelated conversation." Calling it a coincidence might be an exaggeration, but I don't want to give Twyla the satisfaction of being right about my snooping. "I know you think I'm a bored busybody who inserts herself in other people's business, but that's not entirely true."

Twyla's hands freeze, and she looks at me.

"Not *entirely* true?" She smirks, amused at her own observation. "You admit you're a bored busybody, and it's at least part of your motivation." She chuckles, picking up my tote bag and dumps the contents onto the bed. "Who needs this many knitting needles?" she asks under her breath. "Two hands should mean two knitting needles… right?" She holds up the two-point-two-five-millimetre, thirty-two-inch circular needles. "What the?" she mutters. "And so much yarn. Why?" she whispers, creasing her forehead and appraising the small yarn collection scattered across the bed.

"I like to have multiple projects to choose from," I say, defensive of my excessive knitting accessories. "Please don't drop any stitches."

Twyla glares at me like I'm speaking a foreign language.

"The needles in your hand are for knitting in the round."

She looks at me and blinks twice.

"For knitting tubes," I explain. She scans the yarn and knitting notions again. "I own a knitting store. Of course I have a lot of knitting stuff," I say, as a last attempt to justify the contents of my bag.

Ignoring my comment, Twyla feels around inside the empty bag, then inspects it with her flashlight before examining the contents one at a time and returning them to the bag.

"I disagree with the *bored* part of your assessment," I clarify as Twyla abandons my tote bag and steps toward me on her way to the minibar. I step backward out of her way and step on Hannah's foot as she films over my shoulder. I mutter an apology to my daughter, then chase Twyla to the minibar with Hannah limping behind me, aiming her phone at the police officer. "I am a bit of a busybody," I confess. "It's a small-town quirk. That's how we are in Harmony Lake." I shrug. "Everybody knows everybody. We care about each other and look out for one another. We stick our noses in each other's business. Small towns have boundary issues. At least my small town does."

"I knew you were from a small town as soon as I met you. You give off small-town, middle-class, and meddlesome vibes," she says. "You don't have to tell me about small towns and boundary issues, Megan." Twyla slams the minibar shut and moves on to the closet, pulling the spare linens and pillows off the high shelf, shaking each one in case I've hidden the key inside the perfectly folded sheets or between the down pillow and cotton pillowcase. "I grew up in a small town. I'm an expert on the small-town mentality."

Does Twyla hate me because I remind her of the small-town people she grew up with? Did her experience growing up in a small town leave her wounded and now she's bleeding—metaphorically—on me?

"I'm sorry if I represent everything you hate about

small towns," I say. "My goal isn't to antagonize you, Twyla. I want to solve Summer's murder so you can cross Hannah and me off the suspect list. You and I have the same goal. We both want you to solve Summer's murder and arrest her killer. If I find out something useful, isn't that a good thing? I'm trying to help, not be a nuisance."

"Yet you are a nuisance."

Shaking my head, I turn to Hannah's phone and throw my hands in the air with a huff.

"You tried," Hannah mouths, then gives me a sympathetic smile before re-focussing her phone on Twyla as she removes the rod from the closet and shines her flashlight inside, searching for the key she thinks I hid there.

CHAPTER 22

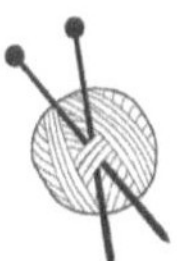

"She's turning over the room next door now," Connie says when she returns from April and Tamara's room.

Twyla finished searching our hotel room and, satisfied that I'm not hiding the key to sauna three, moved along to her next search.

Hannah opens her mouth to say something, but Connie interrupts before she utters a syllable.

"Don't worry," Connie reassures Hannah, "I told Rachel to record every move Twyla makes. I even told her to say what you did at the beginning, where you name all the people who are present, record their faces, and advise us you're filming."

"Thank you." Hannah smiles, and her shoulders drop.

Twyla put everything back *where* she found it, but not *how* she found it. I go through my belongings, checking and adjusting each item.

"Are you all right, my dear?" Connie asks.

"I think so." I nod with a light sigh. "I didn't expect to feel violated by a police search. Twyla touched everything. Even my underwear and the emergency tampons in my purse."

"She was doing her job," Connie reminds me. "I'm sure she didn't enjoy it either. Though she could have been more pleasant. Touching strangers' personal effects must be uncomfortable, even if it is her job."

I'm sure Connie is right. Twyla might dislike me, but I don't feel like she harasses me. Whenever she's nearby, I get the sense Twyla would rather be anywhere other than in my presence.

"I wish I could talk to Eric," I say.

"It must be hard not to have contact with him," Connie sympathizes. "You are newlyweds, after all. I'm sure he misses you just as much as you miss him."

"Yeah," I agree. "I miss him a lot. Right now, I miss his access to the police database. He could make inquiries about Summer's history in the witness protection program. It's too coincidental that someone murdered her almost as soon as she resurfaced, using her old identity and reclaiming her old life. Also, Eric could help me with Twyla. How should I approach her? I don't care if she likes me. I just want her to be less hostile and not write off everything I say as the blathering of a bored busybody."

"Nooooo!" a woman's voice shouts from somewhere down the hall.

"What was that?" I look back and forth between Connie and Hannah, who both shrug.

"It's not mine! I've never seen it before!"

"That's the same voice," Hannah hisses.

"It's coming from the hall," Connie says.

Hannah heads for the door with her phone poised to record.

Curious faces and craned necks line both sides of the third-floor hallway.

"I swear I've never seen it before," Billie pleads, her eyes wide and her hands trembling.

"Then how did it get inside the lining of your suitcase?" Twyla asks, holding a shiny silver key between her gloved thumb and forefinger.

"How can I explain how the key got there if I didn't put it there?" Billie asks. "You're the cop. Aren't you supposed to figure out how it got there?"

"I assume Twyla found the key for sauna three," April whispers as we creep toward each other along the wall between our rooms, meeting in the middle.

"In Billie's stuff?" I ask.

"Looks like it," April replies.

"Anyone could've…"

"I'm sorry, Megan." Twyla glowers at me. "Is my investigation interrupting your conversation?" she barks, calling me out in front of everyone. "Do you have something you'd like to add? I'm sure everyone would love to hear it!" She gestures at the onlookers.

Maria taps Twyla's shoulder, and Twyla turns to look at her. Maria shakes her head. With her customer-service focussed attitude, I'm sure Maria won't tolerate Twyla's rudeness to guests.

I clear my throat.

"Someone else could have planted the key," I say. "Didn't Autumn lose her room key earlier?"

"That's right," Connie says. "Autumn and another guest bumped into each other and spilled their bags, commingling their belongings. The other guest accidentally left with Autumn's room key. Maria had to let Autumn into her room."

"This wouldn't happen if you put room numbers on the keys," Hannah adds.

"Thank you for the observation, ladies," Twyla says with an exaggerated, artificial smile. "Very helpful."

I roll my eyes and shake my head at her sarcastic comment.

"I don't have the key anymore," the doctor calls from down the hall. "I returned it to Maria when she found me and explained the confusion."

That's at least four people, aside from Billie, who could have planted the key: Autumn, Maria, the doctor, and Twyla.

"Key?" asks a curious guest.

"What key?" asks another guest.

"There's a missing key?"

"Whose key?"

"Key for what?"

The chatter of the guests grows louder as they migrate away from their doors and gather in small groups. The employee by the elevator seems unaffected, still cross-legged, still leafing through magazines. I wonder if she saw anyone other than Billie and Autumn enter their room?

"Excuse me!" Twyla shouts over the din of the crowd. "We need to keep the hall clear. Please return to your rooms, continue downstairs for dinner, or go somewhere else. Until further notice, this hallway is for walking through, not standing in. Do your socializing and gossiping elsewhere."

The chatter increases in volume again as guests make hasty arrangements to meet elsewhere. Then at least a dozen doors bang and thud as guests do as they're told and return to their rooms.

"Well, this should make for interesting dinner conversation!" Connie declares.

CHAPTER 23

Sunday, May 8th

As my eyes adjust to the darkness, I remember I'm not at home. This isn't my bed. I'm at the SoulSpring Spa and Retreat.

"Hannah?" I whisper, wiping the sleep from my eyes. "I just had the strangest dream."

I stretch my arm in search of Hannah but find her empty pillow instead.

Where is she?

A *hiss* from my right. Pipes? I prop myself up on my elbows and scan the darkness for clues. The door to Connie's room is closed and dark. The bathroom door is closed, and a strip of light shines through the bottom. Hannah!

I fumble for the lamp on the nightstand, then remember that we unplugged it to save electricity. We weren't sure how much electricity a bedside lamp consumes when it's plugged in, and we couldn't ask the internet, so we erred on the side of caution and unplugged even the most useful modern conveniences.

As I feel my way through the unfamiliar room, the hissing gets louder.

"Dad! I hope you get this!" Hannah whispers as I'm about to tap on the door.

Dad? Adam lives and works in Harmony Lake. He's not in there with Hannah, which can only mean one thing…

"Service!" I declare. "You're talking to Dad?" I gasp as Hannah throws open the bathroom door. "You have service?" I stare at the phone pressed against her ear.

With the glow from the vanity lights around the mirror lighting my way, I rush to the nightstand where my phone is charging.

"I got a text," Hannah explains, following me with her phone still pressed to her ear. "It was from Dad." She pulls the phone away from her ear and looks at the screen. "No service again." She releases a heavy sigh and drops her phone on the bed. "I couldn't sleep," Hannah explains. "I was tossing and turning when the screen lit up. At first, I thought I imagined it. Like, people lost in the desert imagining a Starbucks, or a waterfall, or whatever."

"A mirage?" I ask. "You thought your flashing phone was a mirage?"

"I think she means hallucination," Connie interjects, tying the belt of her bathrobe.

"Right," Hannah says. "I thought I was hallucinating. Hallucinations are a symptom of cell phone withdrawal, right?" She looks back and forth from me to Connie. "I don't know for sure because I can't check the internet. But since we lost cell service, Rachel and I keep hearing our cell phones ring or feeling them vibrate in our pockets. But it's just our imaginations. But this time it was real. It wasn't a hallucination. I got a text from Dad." She picks up her phone from the bed and unlocks it, turning it toward me. "See?"

Dad: Help is coming. Call me as soon as you have cell service. I love you, Princess. Followed by a heart emoji, a crown emoji, and a happy face emoji.

The time stamp is today at 2:14 a.m.

Below Adam's message to Hannah is her response.

Hannah: Hi Dad! I love you too. Followed by a heart emoji and a smiley face emoji.

Time stamp is today at 2:16 a.m.

Under Hannah's response is a small red triangle with a red exclamation point inside.

"Does this mean your reply didn't go through?" I ask, pointing at the foreboding little icon.

Hannah nods.

"I lost service again before it got through." She smiles sadly. "I didn't want to wake you, so I took my phone into the bathroom and stared at it, hoping it would work again."

"Did it?" I ask.

"A few minutes after my failed text to Dad, my phone rang. It was him. I lost service again before I could say hello. He must've tried to call me because he saw I had read his text message."

"But I heard you talking to him," I say.

"I called him back. It went straight to voicemail. I talked fast because I didn't know how much time I would have. I told him about the storm, Summer's murder, the poison we found, and about Twyla treating us like suspects."

She shakes her head and looks at her phone like it's the most disappointing cell phone in existence. "My phone says, *No Service* again. I don't know when I lost the call. Maybe he'll get the entire message, maybe only a bit." She shrugs. "Maybe none."

"Let's hope he gets it," I say, pulling my daughter into a hug. "As soon as the road is safe enough, we're out of here," I assure her, rubbing her back. "I don't care what time of day it is." I pick up my phone. 2:42 a.m. and I have a text notification from Eric.

"I have a missed text!" I unlock my phone. The words *No Service* span the top right corner of the screen where the signal strength should be.

Eric: Hey babe! Help will arrive soon. Call me as soon as you get service. Day or night. I love you. Followed by multiple heart emojis in multiple colours.

"They must be close to restoring our cellular service," Connie says. "I'll be right back. I want to check my phone."

Connie turns and disappears into her dark bedroom. I plug in the lamp on the nightstand and turn it on.

———

TERRIFIED OF MISSING a fleeting window of precious 5G data, we don't go back to bed. Instead, we knock on the door that connects our adjoining rooms and wake up April, Tamara, and Rachel. They discover missed texts from their son Zach and don't go back to bed either. We sit together in exhausted anticipation, constantly monitoring our phones for signs of life and checking the battery strength.

When I comment on how fast my phone battery drains, despite not using it, Hannah and Rachel explain that the lack of cell service and Wi-Fi doesn't mean our phones aren't using any battery. In fact, according to them, the opposite is true. The phone's constant search for an available signal drains the battery faster than normal use with a stable signal. This is the same logic behind our decision to unplug everything in our rooms.

"Happy Mother's Day, ladies," Connie announces as the light of dawn casts a soft glow in the room.

"Happy Mother's Day," we respond with the same enthusiasm as five exhausted sloths.

We pass the next few minutes hugging and exchanging cards. Hannah gives cards to Connie and me, then she gives me a card from Adam. Rachel gives cards to April, Tamara, and Connie. Then, April, Tamara, and I give cards to Connie.

I forgot today is Mother's Day. The entire point of this weekend was to spend time together, celebrating the special women in our lives and the deep connections we share. Instead, we're stranded in luxury accommodation, halfway up a mountain, with a murderer, fighting to prove our innocence and hoping Twyla arrests Summer's killer before they claim another victim. 184

CHAPTER 24

Tamara and Connie went to the Epicurean Bistro to claim a rare and coveted window seat.

"All the best tables will be taken," Connie lamented to encourage Tamara to hurry and get dressed. "I want to enjoy the view while we eat. I refuse to sit by the buffet again. Did you notice people walk faster toward the food than away from it?"

Motivated by our brief contact with the outside world, Hannah and Rachel gathered their homemade antennae and went for a pre-breakfast trek farther up the mountain—again—in search of a signal.

April and I retreat to our respective rooms to shower and get dressed before we join everyone for breakfast.

My cell phone is on the counter, screen up, plugged into the outlet near the sink. Every so often, I glance at it, in case we get another surprise surge of 5G service.

I work the conditioner through my hair, twist it, and

pile the long, wet mound on top of my head. I rinse the conditioner from my hands and wipe a circle on the shower door, clearing it enough to peek at my phone.

It's moving.

The screen is flashing and the phone spins in slow circles on the marble countertop.

Don't hang up, Eric!

I step out of the shower, and Eric's face flashes on the screen. Dripping wet, I unlock the phone, leaving it on the counter.

"Eric?!" Water drips from my face onto the screen.

I dry my hand on a nearby towel and put the phone on speaker so I don't have to hold it against my wet head. "Hello?!"

"It's so good to hear your voice!" Eric exhales like he held his breath too long. "Are you OK, babe? Gawd, I miss you! How about Hannah and everyone else? Is everyone OK?"

"We're fine," I say. "How are you? How's Zach? April and T are so worried..."

"Zach's fine," Eric interrupts me. "He's with me. I invited him to stay here when we lost touch with you guys."

"Thank you," I say. "Tell him his mums and sister are fine."

"They can tell him themselves," Eric says. "Zach's right here."

While I wrap myself in a towel and barge into the adjoining suite through the connecting door, Eric tells me Adam was worried about Hannah, and Archie was worried about Connie, so he invited them to stay at our house too.

"It made sense to wait together," Eric says. "If one of us heard anything or contacted you, we would all be here."

"Where did everyone sleep?" I ask.

"Sophie and I were in our room, Adam slept in Hannah's room, and Archie and Zach shared the spare room."

"Sounds like quite the slumber party," I tease.

April emerges from the bedroom, and I hand her my phone.

While April enjoys the best Mother's Day gift possible, hearing her seventeen-year-old son's voice after being unable to reach him for almost thirty-six hours, I rush back to the shower and rinse the conditioner out of my hair.

Worried the data connection won't last, I set a new speed record drying off and getting dressed.

Clothed but with my hair wrapped in a towel, I emerge from the bathroom. April holds the phone out to me.

"Eric?"

"Happy Mother's Day, Meg!"

"Oh. Adam. Hi," I say, hoping my voice doesn't betray my shock. "Hannah's fine. She's not with me now, but I promise she's healthy and unharmed," I assure him. "Except for the emotional pain and inconvenience of not having a cell phone. I'm so sorry. I can't imagine how worried you've been."

As much as I'd prefer not to be stranded with limited modern conveniences in forced proximity to a killer, I wouldn't switch places with my ex-husband for anything. At least I know where Hannah is. I know she's safe, and I can keep an eye on her. I can't imagine not knowing and not being able to contact her. The past day-and-a-half must have been torture for Adam.

"I spoke with her," he says. "She called me from somewhere outside the spa. We spoke until her phone cut out," he says. "We figured you were all right. A helicopter flew over the spa yesterday, and the pilot reported that everything appeared fine. Also, Eric got hold of a satellite image of the spa after the storm."

"You know more than us," I say.

"I'm glad you're OK, Meg. I'm glad everyone is OK."

"Thanks."

"I'll hand the phone back to Eric," he says.

"Hey, babe."

I can hear the smile in Eric's voice.

"Hi!" I gush.

"Are you alone, babe?"

April uses hand motions to tell me she's going back to her room to finish getting ready. I nod in response.

"I am now," I reply after April closes the connecting door.

"Tell me about this murder."

"You know about Summer's murder?"

Adam received part of the voicemail Hannah left for him at 2:41 a.m. He played the partial message for Eric. The message ended mid-sentence, but after Hannah mentioned the storm, the power failure, the cell phone service failure, and Summer's murder.

"What's Twyla's last name?" Eric asks after I tell him about the baggie of spotted water hemlock, Twyla's investigation, and Hannah and I featuring on Twyla's suspect list.

"Proudfoot," I reply.

Eric repeats the name, drawing out each syllable like he's writing it down.

"Twyla hates me, honey," I say. "She thinks I'm an interfering busy body."

"You're a helpful, interfering busy body with good instincts," Eric assures me.

"She has a personal relationship with a suspect," I disclose. "And I can't verify her alibi."

"You can't verify whose alibi?"

"Twyla's," I clarify. "Actually, no one's. I can't verify any alibis."

"Why would the investigator need an alibi?" he asks with a chuckle.

I explain to Eric about Twyla's sudden arrival just before the power went out. I tell him how Twyla and Maria were unaccounted for when the killer lured the sauna attendant away while they sneaked into sauna three, moved Summer's body, locked the door, and stole the key.

"She searched our room for the missing key," I say. "Can she do that without a warrant?"

Eric says it sounds like Twyla's search was legal, but he wants to view Hannah's video footage.

"Be careful, babe."

"Always."

"Stay together. Don't eat or drink anything that looks or smells weird or you aren't familiar with. Try to stick with pre-packaged food and drinks."

"OK."

This would be a bad time to mention Nadira's culinary accomplishments and all the new foods I've tried this weekend.

"Adam is in contact with the mayor up there, and I'm in contact with the local police chief," Eric says. "They assure us the road will be clear sometime tomorrow. Crews have been working on it since yesterday morning."

"Honey, what do you know about the witness protection program?" I ask, changing the subject.

"Federal or provincial?"

"There are multiple witness protection programs?" I ask. "I'm not sure."

I tell him about Autumn's disclosure, that her sister's testimony helped convict a killer.

"I can't promise anything, but I'll look into it," Eric says.

"Thank you," I say. "I miss you and Sophie. Tell me all the news from Harmony Lake."

Eric distracts me with tales of how much Sophie

loves having a house full of guests. He says she's convinced they're there to provide laps for her to sit on, give her treats, and take her for walks. Then he tells me that one of his officers is retiring next month after forty years of service.

"I have less than a month to plan his retirement party and hire his replacement," Eric says with a sigh.

"I can help with the retirement party," I offer. "Everyone in town knows him and will want to help. I'll put it on project status when I get home."

"Thank you," he says. "If you can also send out a job posting, sort through the applications, arrange interviews, conduct interviews, choose an applicant, then make them an offer, that would be great too."

"Ummm, I can help with the retirement party." We laugh. "But I'll keep my eyes and ears open for potential candidates."

———

WITHIN SECONDS of taking our seats, a server carrying a tray of mango mimosas wishes April and me Happy Mother's Day and places a champagne flute in front of each of us.

"Some guests have intermittent cellular service, and some have no cellular service," Connie updates us after we raise our glasses and toast each other.

April and I tell everyone about our conversation with Zach, Eric, and Adam. Tamara also had a brief conversation with their son, and Rachel tells us that she exchanged texts with Zack while she and Hannah wandered nearby hiking trails. Connie had a brief conversation with her partner, Archie, but the signal dropped, and she hasn't had service since. Hannah spoke with Adam, then her boyfriend, but her signal only lasts about two minutes at a time, with long gaps in between.

April and I join the buffet line and look at the other guests' full plates as they walk back to their tables. We deliberate about what to sample first. Someone's cell phone dings, and the rest of us whip out our phones.

"No service," I say, checking my phone.

"Me neither," April says.

"I haven't had service since Eric phoned earlier. We got disconnected right after he told me one of his officers is retiring next month."

"Who?"

I tell her the retiring officer's name—she knows him and his family because everyone knows everyone else in Harmony Lake—and we brainstorm ideas for his retirement party while we inch forward in line.

"Artsy Tartsy will do the cake, of course," she offers, referring to her and Tamara's bakery. "I'll call his wife when we get home and work out the details."

A server hands me a warm plate. I thank her and scan the long table of food in front of me.

"There's so much to choose from," I comment. "What should we try first?"

"This place goes all out for Mother's Day brunch," April concurs.

We agree to divide and conquer, choosing different items so we can share when we get back to the table. I load my plate with maple glazed breakfast sausage, banana bread pancakes, and bite-size spinach and ham egg tarts. As I make my way from dish to dish, Nadira emerges from the kitchen and, smiling, takes a visual inventory of the buffet. Her pride is well deserved. We make eye contact, and she gives me a thumbs-up.

"Amazing," I mouth to her, then make a chef's kiss.

April chooses a ham and cheese croissant with honey mustard glaze, smoked salmon puff pastry nests, and eggs Benedict with avocado spread and tomato slices.

"Nadira has outdone herself," Tamara comments, then sips her strawberry and sparkling wine punch.

"Who else is ready for another trip to the buffet?" Connie asks, laying her napkin on the table and standing up.

"This will be my third trip," I say, finishing the last bite of crepe with strawberries and lemon curd. "But I need to try the ham biscuits with apricot mustard."

I dab my mouth with my napkin and join Connie at the end of the buffet line.

"Oh, look! There's Billie," Connie says, pointing her chin toward the end of the buffet.

Billie's back is toward us, but her ginger hair makes her easy to recognize. I catch occasional glimpses of her face as she slides her empty plate along the buffet.

"I wonder what happened yesterday after Twyla evicted everyone from the third-floor hallway?"

"There's only one way to find out, my dear," Connie replies.

"I don't see Autumn," I say, scanning the tables. "Do you think Billie is alone? Maybe we should invite her to join us."

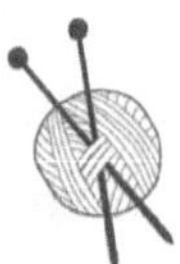

CHAPTER 25

"Billie!"

She stops and looks around.

I speed up, closing the distance between us before she walks away.

"Oh. Hi, Megan," Billie says with a small smile.

"Hi," I say, closing the last few feet between us. "How are you? I've been thinking about you since Twyla found the key in your room yesterday."

"I'm fine," Billie assures me. "I don't know how it got there. I swear, I had never even seen the key before. Twyla made it clear she thinks I killed Summer."

"There are several suspects in Summer's murder," I say, hoping to ease her mind. "Myself included."

"At least I'm in good company," she says with a weak smile. "I can't stand being stranded with Summer's murderer. What if they get away with it? What if the police don't figure out who killed her?" Billie glances at her plate, then looks away as though it offended her. "It makes my stomach turn. I'm sure it's part of the reason I feel like this."

Her plate is empty except for a small slice of quiche Lorraine.

"Summer's killer won't get away," I say with more confidence than I feel.

"Happy Mother's Day."

"Thank you," I say, surprised by the sentiment.

I realize I don't know if Billie or the twins are mothers. None of them have mentioned kids, but that doesn't mean they don't have any.

"Do you or the twins have kids?" I ask.

"No," Billie replies, shaking her head. "Not yet. My husband and I hope to start our family this year. For the first half of the year, we're focussing on our physical and mental health. That's why we came here. Autumn and Summer thought it would be a good way to keep me motivated."

"Good for you," I congratulate her.

"My husband and I are working on making healthier food choices and learning to manage our stress better."

"It sounds like you're making positive changes," I say.

"I'm trying," Billie says. "It's difficult to make healthy food choices when I can't keep anything down and have trouble staying awake until sunset. It's hard to manage stress when one of my best friends gets murdered."

"Would you like to join us?" I ask, gesturing behind

me. "We have a huge table by the window, and we'd love to have brunch with you."

Billie looks at the slice of quiche on her plate and crinkles her nose.

"I don't think so," she says. "Thank you for asking, though. I'm not sure I'll finish this piece of quiche, and the smell of food makes my nausea worse."

"Is that why you were late for roll call on Friday night?" I ask. "Were you sick?"

Billie nods. "After my massage, dinner made a reappearance. I went upstairs to lie down. When Autumn and Summer didn't come back, I looked for them. An employee asked me to join everyone in the bistro."

Autumn told me she was lying in their hotel room because of her migraine symptoms. How did Autumn and Billie miss each other? Is Billie lying? Is Autumn lying? Are they both lying?

"Wasn't Autumn in your room too? Resting because she had a migraine?"

"We figure we missed each other," Billie explains. "I must have gone upstairs after Autumn left to search for me and Summer. Then, she must have come back to check the room after I left to look for her and Summer."

"You didn't hear the knock at your door when Maria dispatched employees to herd the guests for roll call?"

"No one knocked at our door while I was there."

Billie turns up her nose and straightens her arms, maximizing the distance between her nose and the quiche.

"It's too bad you're so sick," I say, recalling Logan,

the massage therapist's observation that the aroma of the incense also made Billie nauseous. "Have you always had a physical reaction to scents and aromas?"

"No," Billie replies. "I think it's a side effect of this stomach bug. It makes me sleepy all the time and certain smells make the nausea worse."

"I can relate," I sympathize. "I had a similar bug years ago. Same symptoms. Rolling nausea, hypersensitive sense of smell, chronic fatigue…"

"How long did it last?" Billie asks, interrupting my inventory of symptoms.

Before I can reply, Nadira approaches us, smiling and carrying a tray.

"Hi, Billie. I'm glad I caught you," she says.

"You're looking for me?" Billie asks after Nadira and I greet each other.

"I saw you in the buffet line. You seemed uncomfortable. I assume you were searching for something that would be easy on your stomach."

Billie nods and glances at her quiche Lorraine which is starting to look cold and dry.

"I thought this might help." Nadira holds up the tray and nods toward the thermos. "Chamomile tea to help with indigestion and nausea," she explains, then nods toward the white ceramic ramekin. "Ginger lozenges to help relieve nausea." She nods at the bowl next to it. "Applesauce to help settle your stomach." She nods at the plate. "And soda crackers and a banana."

"That's so thoughtful," Billie says, her eyes welling with moisture. "Thank you."

A bit of an emotional response on Billie's part, but she's going through a lot of emotional upheaval right now. Nadira holds out the tray, and Billie looks at the plate she's carrying, figuring out how to carry everything.

"Give me the quiche," I say, relieving Billie of the tray.

"You guys are amazing." A single tear rolls down Billie's cheek. "I don't know what to say. This weekend has been so overwhelming."

Nadira softens at Billie's emotional reaction to her thoughtful gesture. "Why don't we sit for a minute."

Nadira places a hand on Billie's shoulder and leads us to a nearby door, ushering us through, ahead of her. This must be Nadira's office. Like Maria's office, it has two doors. I assume the other door leads to the kitchen.

Nadira takes the tray from Billie and sets it on the desk, easing Billie into an armchair. Then, she takes the plate of quiche Lorraine from me and places it on a table behind the desk and gestures for me to sit in the armchair next to Billie's.

"I'm sorry," Billie says, sniffling. "I'm just so sad and tired and sick. Feeling lousy is exhausting."

"No need to apologize," Nadira assures her. "Do what you need to do. If you need to cry"—she shrugs—"you cry. Suppressing it does more harm than good. Crying relieves anxiety. Tears contain stress hormones. You're helping your body eliminate stress when you cry. Crying also causes fatigue, which may be why you're so tired."

"You know a lot about crying," Billie says with a sniffle.

"I am an Ayurvedic practitioner," Nadira explains, "and in the Ayurvedic tradition, we believe that suppressing tears leads to physical and mental symptoms."

I suspect something else is behind Billie's physical symptoms, but I don't mention it because Nadira's explanation makes sense and her calm, reassuring words help Billie relax.

"The foods on this tray are gentle for your stomach," Nadira explains. "And they don't require refrigeration or special storage. You can nibble at them throughout the day."

"I'll try," Billie smiles. "Thank you."

"Maybe the lamb chop you ordered yesterday was too rich for your stomach right now," Nadira suggests.

"I didn't order the lamb chop," Billie says. "Autumn ordered it for me. I couldn't eat very much. I ate most of the rice and broccoli that you served with it, though. It was delicious, I just couldn't stomach it."

Billie's comment gives me pause, and judging by the momentary confusion on Nadira's face, it gives her pause too. While Nadira shakes off the dissonance and explains to Billie reasons to consider avoiding animal products until her stomach feels better, I recall the meat-less lamb chop bone outside Billie's room.

The door to the kitchen swings open.

"Nadira, can we go over next week's food order?" Maria asks, then looks up from the clipboard in her hand. "Oh. Hello, Billie. Hello, Megan." She smiles, nudging the bridge of her glasses with her spare hand. "How is everyone today?"

Pots and pans clanging in the kitchen make it difficult to hear her.

"Fine," we mumble almost in sync.

"Megan, I'm glad I bumped into you. Twyla would like to speak with you. Are you available after brunch?"

"Sure," I reply. "I was going to visit you later, anyway, and ask you for something. I'm scheduled to have a petrissage scalp massage after brunch, but…"

"Don't worry about that," Maria says, smiling and flicking her wrist. "I'll let them know you'll be late." She smiles again, this time showing all her teeth. "After brunch, in my office?"

"Sure," I say, trying to match her smile.

"I should get going," Billie announces, standing up and collecting the tray from Nadira's desk. "I don't like to leave Autumn alone longer than necessary." She hoists the tray to shoulder height. "Thank you again, Chef." She smiles. "And thanks for checking in with me, Megan."

"I should leave too," I say, standing up. "My family will wonder where I've disappeared to." I open the office door for Billie, and she steps past me and into the hall.

"Megan, can you hang back?" Nadira asks. "I'd like to ask you something."

"Sure." I sit down again.

"You two talk," Maria says. "Nadira, we can go over the food order later. Megan, I saw your family having breakfast. I'll let them know where you are, so they won't worry."

"Thanks," I say before Maria disappears into the kitchen. "What's up?" I ask Nadira.

"Be careful when you talk to Twyla and Maria," she warns in a whisper. "Take someone with you." She arches a perfectly shaped eyebrow. "A witness."

"Why?" I ask. "Do you know why Twyla wants to talk to me?"

"I don't know why they want to talk to you," Nadira whispers, leaning across the desk and shooting a quick glance at the kitchen door. "But something is going on. Maria and Twyla are more uptight than usual."

"Summer's murder is stressing out everyone."

"It's more than that." She narrows her gaze and shakes her head slowly. "I can't put my finger on it." She sighs. "Twyla hardly ever visits Maria at work. But she was here Wednesday, Thursday, and Friday."

"Interesting," I say. "Why?"

"I don't know," Nadira replies. "But something else weird is going on." She moves her index finger in a come-hither motion, so I lean toward the desk. "Maria and Summer had two intense discussions between the time Summer checked in on Wednesday and her death on Friday night."

"Intense?" I ask. "Did you overhear anything?"

"I couldn't get close enough to eavesdrop, but they

were huddled together in a corner near the yoga studio on Wednesday afternoon, and on Friday morning, they were talking near the front desk. When Maria caught me watching them on Friday, she took Summer into her office."

"Are you sure Maria was talking with Summer?" I ask. "You admitted you couldn't tell Autumn and Summer apart."

"Trust me, it was Summer," Nadira insists. "I'm sure it was Summer because when I saw them outside the yoga studio, I watched Maria and Summer over Autumn's shoulder. Autumn was accusing me of poisoning Billie. And on Friday, Autumn and Billie were having breakfast when Maria and Summer had their heads together at the front desk. I was looking for Maria. I wanted to warn her about the accusations Autumn was slinging at me and tell her that Autumn threatened to take the accusations public."

"Did Maria and Summer appear friendly?" I ask. "Did they laugh and act familiar with each other?"

"The opposite," Nadira replies. "Summer cried during both conversations, and Maria cried outside the yoga studio. It wasn't angry crying. It was more like sad crying. Like they were sharing sad stories or something."

"What could Maria and Summer have discussed that made them emotional?" I wonder out loud.

"I don't know," Nadira replies. "But I saw Twyla give you the stink-eye on the back deck yesterday near the lounge chairs, and I heard how she chastised you in the third-floor hallway yesterday evening. I thought I should give you a heads-up."

"Thanks for the warning," I say.

The gossip network at the SoulSpring Spa and Retreat rivals the Harmony Lake gossip network.

CHAPTER 26

"Thanks for coming with me," I say.

"Of course, I came with you!" April declares. "I'm dying to know why they want to talk to you."

"Please don't joke about dying," I say, forcing my face to stay serious.

We burst out laughing.

"Do you think the baggie is still there?" April asks, pointing to the filing cabinet where Twyla locked up the potential poison.

"I hope so," I say, just as Maria's office door opens.

"Thanks for coming, Megan." Maria smiles, then greets April with the same optimism and bright smile.

Twyla follows Maria into the office.

"Hello, ladies," she mutters, nodding and making brief eye contact with us before looking away.

"Hello," April and I respond.

Twyla leans against the back of the door, her shoulders stooped. She picks at the skin around her thumb.

Physically, she looks the same as yesterday, but her energy and mood are different. Somehow, Twyla takes up less space than last time the four of us were assembled in Maria's office. Her presence is less imposing, and the atmosphere is lighter than it usually is when Twyla is around.

"Megan," Maria says, wheeling her chair toward her desk and straightening her spine. "Twyla has something she'd like to say to you." She laces her fingers together on the desk and looks at the law enforcement officer. "Don't you, Twyla?"

"I'm sorry for yelling at you in the hallway yesterday in front of the other guests," Twyla mumbles, looking at me.

"I'd like to apologize too, Megan," Maria says. "We strive to treat every guest and employee at the Soul-Spring Spa and Retreat with the utmost respect and courtesy."

"Thank you," I say, taken aback by the apologies. "I'm sorry if my whispering interfered with your investigation."

"This… situation is stressful for all of us, but it's especially stressful for Twyla—"

"Because I'm the only law enforcement officer here," Twyla says, cutting off Maria mid-sentence.

"I understand," I say, smiling. "Do you mind if we go to our petrissage scalp massage now?"

April and I rise to our feet.

"I remembered where I'd seen your husband before!" Maria announces.

April and I sit back down.

"I told you it would come to me as soon as you left my office, and that's what happened."

"Oh?" I ask.

"He was a keynote speaker at the police conference Twyla attended last month." Maria opens her desk drawer. "I found the itinerary Twyla brought home from the conference. It includes a photo and biography of each speaker." She hands me the brochure. "Your husband's photo is the same photo you showed me on your phone yesterday. Him and your dog, Sophie."

"So, it is." I smile and pass the brochure to April.

"Twyla said his speech was her favourite part of the conference," Maria gushes.

"That's quite a compliment," I respond.

"I learned a lot from his talk about how social media impacts policing in small communities," Twyla adds. "It was really informative."

"I will tell him." I smile.

"I realized you were Chief Sloane's wife when I interviewed you in the sauna," Twyla adds, swallowing. "I panicked because I knew you had helped him solve a few cases. Chief Sloane has a stellar reputation as a murder investigator. I would hate if he based his first impression of my investigative skills on this case, under these circumstances."

Twyla inhales and fidgets with her fingers, shifting her weight from one foot to the other. "I freaked out. I was sure you could tell this was my first murder investigation. Summer's murder was the first murder scene

I'd ever attended, and I didn't want it to be obvious. You've attended more murder scenes than me, and you're a civilian. I worried you would tell Chief Sloane that I'm inexperienced and incompetent. Then he would tell my chief, and I'd never get promoted or get hired somewhere else."

"Yesterday when I remembered where I'd seen your husband, I told Twyla, and she admitted she had already figured it out. Then she told me why she was avoiding you," Maria adds.

"I see," I say. "Twyla, I couldn't tell this was your first murder. You exude so much confidence and authority, that I assumed you were a seasoned investigator."

"Maybe I'm a better actor than cop." Twyla laughs and her facial muscles soften. She straightens her spine, pulling herself up a little taller. "This is a small town. We've never had a murder here. Until this weekend, the biggest crime I had ever investigated was a string of bicycle thefts from the local high school." She laughs. "I don't want to sound cold, but Summer's murder is an opportunity for me. This is my chance to prove I can preserve a crime scene, collect evidence, interview witnesses... to prove I would be a good detective."

"I keep telling her she's doing a great job"—Maria shakes her head—"but she won't listen."

"I'm sure your boss, and everyone else, will be impressed. You're very professional," April adds.

"I bet if your boss shows up tomorrow and you

hand him a short list of suspects, or better yet, a cuffed suspect, it would impress him," I comment.

"Yes, it would," Twyla confirms. "It would look great on my resume too." Something buzzes, and Twyla grabs the cell phone on her hip. "Excuse me, I have to take this."

April, Maria, and I grab our phones and check for service. Nothing. We sigh and put our phones down, frustrated by the fickle data connection.

"Thank you again for coming," Maria says after Twyla leaves the office. "And thank you for understanding."

"No problem," I say. "Can I ask you something?"

"Sure," Maria says.

"What did you and Summer discuss in private?"

"What are you talking about?" Maria squeezes her eyebrows together under the rim of her black frames.

"Someone mentioned that you had at least two private conversations with Summer. Conversations that included *sad crying*, to quote my source." I put air quotes around *sad crying*.

"Is Nadira your source?" Maria asks, crossing her arms in front of her chest and shaking her head. "That interfering woman starts most of the gossip in this place. Why can't she stay in the kitchen where she belongs?" She huffs. "If it weren't for all her culinary awards and large following, I would've gotten rid of her ages ago."

April and I exchange subtle, shocked glances. These are the harshest words Maria has said in our presence.

"It doesn't matter who the source is," I say. "What matters is that you had multiple emotional discussions with Summer before her death."

"We talked about Mother's Day brunch," Maria declares. "This was the twins first Mother's Day together without their mother. It was an emotional conversation, and Summer cried, which made me cry. I'm a sympathetic crier. I can't control it." Maria cocks an eyebrow. "Summer wanted to surprise Autumn with the same Mother's Day breakfast they used to make for their mother. She asked if it would be possible to arrange a special, off-menu meal and have room service deliver it."

"What was the meal?" I ask.

"I don't know," Maria replies. "I told her I would discuss her request with the chef and if we could accommodate it, Nadira would reach out to Summer for the details."

"Did you discuss it with Nadira?" April asks.

"I forgot," Maria admits, scrunching up her face in shame. "She asked me the night they checked in, but it slipped my mind until Summer asked me again on Friday. I felt horrible for forgetting. I didn't have time to talk to Nadira about it before Summer died."

"So sad," April says.

"I know," Maria agrees.

"Can I ask you something else?" I ask, changing the subject.

"Of course," Maria says, dabbing the corner of her eye with her thumb.

"Why has Twyla visited you so often since Billie and the twins checked in? I heard she's visited you every day since they arrived, but before that, she rarely visited the spa."

"Twyla's visits have nothing to do with any spa guest," Maria replies. "Remember when I told you Twyla was job hunting?"

I nod.

"She found a few opportunities, and I was helping her with her resume."

"Good luck to her. I hope she gets an interview," I say. "Also, would you have any pregnancy tests?"

"Excuse me?" April and Maria ask, like I asked Maria to give me a grenade.

"A pregnancy test," I reiterate. "They were in the basket with the bandages on Friday night. May I have one please?"

"Of course." Maria stands up and blinks several times in quick succession. "I'll be right back."

"Are you pregnant?" April demands, when Maria leaves.

"I hope not," I reply.

"Does Eric know?"

Before I can answer, Maria returns carrying the basket of toiletries.

"Good luck?" She hands me a long, thin, shrink-wrapped box.

"Thanks." I smile, tucking the test inside my knitting bag.

———

"IF SUMMER WANTED to surprise her sister with a special breakfast, why didn't she ask Nadira? Why did she ask Maria?" April asks on the way to our petrissage scalp massage.

"I wondered the same thing," I admit. "And where was Maria's uncontrollable sympathetic crying response on Friday night when Autumn was sobbing over her sister's death?"

"This doesn't feel right," April concurs. "The key appearing out of nowhere in Billie's suitcase, Maria's secret conversations with the murder victim, Summer's past in the witness protection program, Billie's constant nausea, the baggie of spotted water hemlock stuck between the lounge chair cushions. I feel like it's just a matter of putting the clues in the right order, but no matter how I rearrange them, they don't make sense."

"It's like untangling yarn," I say. "Just when I think I've undone the last knot, and the yarn is tangle-free, I encounter an even bigger knot a few yards later." I sigh. "I never expected Twyla to apologize or admit that she was irritable because she's insecure about her investigative skills."

"Me neither," April agrees. "Is Twyla insecure, or does she think displaying emotional vulnerability will convince you that her behaviour wasn't because she was manipulating evidence?"

"Maybe she hopes I'll forget that she has no verifiable alibi for the time window when the killer likely moved Summer's body."

"Who drives halfway up a mountain three days in a row for resume help?" April asks, pulling the door to the scalp massage area. "Geesh! Just email the resume like a normal person."

So many questions, so few answers.

CHAPTER 27

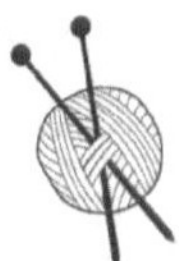

"Red Herring?" I ask Hannah, holding up the bottle of matte vermillion nail polish.

"Good choice," she agrees.

"What shade did you choose?" I ask as we settle into side-by-side pedicure chairs for our Mother's Day Mother-Daughter Mani-Pedi.

"It's called Kiss my A's." She holds up the bottle of neon-pink polish.

"Hi, Megan," a small voice says from the pedicure chair on my other side.

"Autumn!" I force myself to rein in my shock for fear of frightening her away. "It's nice to see you," I say in the same gentle voice I would use to convince a baby animal to leave the safety of its hiding place.

Autumn leans forward and looks around me, greeting Hannah. Hannah returns the greeting and smiles.

"Do you and Hannah visit a spa every Mother's Day?" Autumn asks.

"This is our first time," I reply. "Hannah's dad usually makes brunch for us."

"That's nice," Autumn says. "Tradition is important. My mother loved daisies. Every Mother's Day I would take her for lunch at her favourite restaurant and give her a bouquet of daisies. I always signed Summer's name, even though she wasn't there." Autumn's smile is sad and nostalgic.

"I'm sorry," I say. "Today must be hard. My mum died when Hannah was a baby. Mother's Day is still bittersweet."

"Since my mum died, I still buy daisies on Mother's Day, but now I put them in a vase in my kitchen and let them remind me of her," Autumn says.

"Did you have any Mother's Day traditions before Summer left?" I probe. "Like a handmade card, or a special breakfast, or something?"

"Sure," Autumn replies. "We made Mother's Day cards in school when we were little. But as teenagers, we were too cool for handmade cards, so we bought a card together and both signed it. As for breakfast"—she shakes her head—"Mum never ate breakfast. She had coffee in the morning but didn't eat until lunch."

Why would Maria tell me Summer wanted to arrange a special Mother's Day breakfast just like the one she and Autumn used to make for their mother? Who's lying, Maria or Autumn? Why would Autumn lie? She has nothing to risk by telling me about her family's Mother's Day traditions. Why would Maria lie? Because she doesn't want me to know the truth about what she and Summer discussed during their secret, tearful conversations. What secret is Maria lying to protect?

"How's your migraine?" I ask, aiming for a less emotional topic of conversation.

"I've kept it away so far," Autumn replies, lifting a foot out of the water at the nail technician's prompting.

"That's good," I say.

"It's temporary," Autumn corrects me. "I might have won the battle, but I haven't won the war. I've had migraines since I was eleven years old, and I expect to have them for the rest of my life."

"Did Summer suffer with chronic migraines too?" I ask, wondering if identical twins also share identical chronic health conditions.

"No," Autumn replies, shaking her head. "She had occasional sinus headaches before it would rain, but never migraines."

"Autumn," I say, thinking how sad she must be about marking Mother's Day so soon after her sister's death. "If you want to be alone and would rather not talk, I'll do my best to be quiet," I half joke.

"It's kind of you to offer," Autumn snickers. "I wanted to do something normal today. Getting a pedicure when you're staying at a spa is normal. Later, I might take a normal walk in the garden."

The nail technician taps her leg, and by instinct, Autumn lifts her foot out of the water and rests it on the ledge. "The spa has an extensive herb garden. I'd like to check it out."

"Do you garden?" I ask.

"I wish," Autumn replies. "I used to have a small herb garden, but I don't have time anymore."

"How's Billie feeling?" I ask.

"She's napping," Autumn replies. "These days, she either naps or throws up. She came back to our room with a tray of food prepared by Nadira." Autumn rolls her eyes. "I warned her not to eat it, but she won't listen to me. I don't know what Nadira does to Billie's food, but it's making her sick."

"Speaking of Billie," I say. "I hear she worried about you when Summer came back from the Witness Protection Program."

"Who told you that?" Autumn asks.

"Someone overheard your conversation. She said Billie warned you to be careful trusting Summer again. Why did Billie say that?"

"Your gossipy friend only heard part of the conversation," Autumn says, then inhales a deep breath and lets it out. "My sister was gone for over ten years. A lot happens in a decade. Our mother's constant worry made her sick. Our mother's health got worse, and I took care of her by myself. I made every decision and the final arrangements. Billie supported me, but it's not the same as having a sister to share the burden and share the pain.

"When Mum got too sick, I took over the business. I had to teach myself how to be the boss. It terrified me.

We have dozens of employees who rely on the business to take care of their families. Between caring for Mum and running the business, I didn't have time to hang out with friends, date, or start a family. I feel guilty for admitting it, but I resented Summer for leaving. For over ten years, she didn't have any responsibility. She lived her own life and didn't have to consider anyone else. I can't even imagine what that would feel like."

"It's understandable," I say. "You dealt with a lot by yourself. You handled your mum's illness when she was alive, her affairs after she died, and kept the business successful. It must've been hard when Summer came back and expected half of your mum's share of the business."

"Did your source tell you that too?" Autumn asks.

"I have multiple sources," I admit.

"I was hesitant," Autumn admits. "But Summer and I talked about it. We yelled and cried and worked it out. It turns out Summer felt bad too. She resented me. Summer was jealous that I spent those last years with our mum and she couldn't. She resented me for living in our hometown. She had to build a new life with new people. Her new life was a lie. Summer said every friendship she had in witness protection started with a lie—her name." The nail technician interrupts us to show Autumn her first painted nail, a lovely shade of pale lilac.

Autumn approves the colour, the nail technician continues polishing, and Autumn returns to our conversation.

"Summer's time away made both of us resentful. We were both hurt. Mum would have hated that. She would have wanted Summer to own part of the business. I instructed my lawyer to draw up the paperwork. I planned to surprise Summer with the paperwork next week when we got home."

I guess Summer's death means Autumn will continue to be the sole owner of the family business.

"How did Billie feel about Summer's return?" I ask, grimacing because the nail technician is filing my nails, and it tickles. "Was she jealous about sharing your attention with Summer again?"

"Billie was cautious," Autumn admits. "We hadn't seen or spoken to Summer since we were teenagers. What if she had changed? What if we had changed? I could tell Billie had reservations at first. But when she saw Summer hadn't changed, she was fine. They were both hesitant. Without Summer, Billie and I had each other, but Summer didn't have anyone. I think Summer resented that. Sometimes Billie and I would refer to something or make an inside joke that Summer didn't understand. I could tell she felt sad and left out."

Autumn's nail technician moves her across the salon to a chair with a dryer.

"Is Nadira your source, Mum?" Hannah asks, leaning toward me.

"She's one source," I reply.

"For someone who claims she's always in the kitchen, Nadira sees and hears a lot of stuff."

My daughter makes a good point.

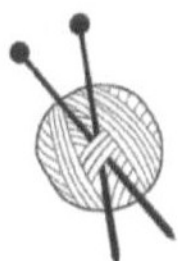

CHAPTER 28

MONDAY, May 9th

The road crew's progress brought them within earshot of the spa just before sunset last night. Buoyed by the prospect of a clear, safe escape route and cell phone service more stable than it has been since before the storm, the collective mood at breakfast is relaxed and optimistic. Smiles are brighter, conversations revolve less around speculation about when we'll be able to leave, and more about planning and packing for the trip home.

"Who are you looking for, my dear?" Connie asks between bites of yogurt-granola-berry parfait. "Are you waiting for someone specific to walk in?"

"Something like that," I admit, sipping my second cup of coffee. "I was hoping Billie would make another appearance today."

"Autumn said Billie is having breakfast in their room," Connie says. "I bumped into her at the buffet.

She said Billie was a sickly shade of green when she woke up."

"Where's Autumn now?" I ask, scanning the tables without missing a stitch on the spa washcloth I'm knitting.

"On the deck," Connie replies. "She fancied eating outside and taking in the view before they leave today. I invited her to join us, but she was in a hurry. She has a hot stone massage right after breakfast."

We have no scheduled spa treatments this morning, so after breakfast we return to our room to pack in anticipation of sleeping in our own beds in Harmony Lake tonight.

"Don't forget, my dear, you wanted to visit the gift shop and pick up some soaps and such to go with the washcloths you knitted," Connie says as we climb the stairs to the third floor.

"Right," I respond. "Thank you for reminding me." As we pass Billie and Autumn's room, I grip my knitting bag and feel the hard corners of the box Maria gave me yesterday. "I think I'll check on Billie," I say, stopping just past their door.

"I'll come with you," Connie offers.

"Thank you, but it's unnecessary. I'll only be a few minutes. You can pack, I'll be fine."

"Are you sure?" Connie narrows her gaze. "We promised to watch each other until Twyla arrests Summer's killer, or we leave this place."

"I'll be right here," I assure her, pointing to Billie

and Autumn's room. "If something happens, I'll scream so loud the road crews will hear me."

"Fine," Connie agrees. "But if you aren't inside our room in fifteen minutes, I'm coming to check on you."

"Deal," I say, watching Connie let herself into our room and lock the door.

I'm about to knock on Billie's door when my phone vibrates and rings inside my knitting bag. It's Eric.

"Hello?" I say, striding down the hall toward the stairwell and out of earshot of the employee loitering near the elevator door.

"Good morning, babe," says my handsome husband. "The road is almost clear. You should be able to leave in a few hours."

"We heard the same thing," I say.

I step inside the stairwell and look down the stairs, making sure I'm alone.

"I can't wait to see you," Eric says. "I'm gonna cuddle you so hard!"

"I could use a good, hard cuddle."

"I did some digging," Eric says. "What do you want to hear first, what I learned about Summer and the witness protection program, or what I learned about Officer Twyla Proudfoot?"

"Summer, please."

"Babe, are you sure about the details? You said Summer was an innocent bystander who risked her safety to testify against a murder suspect, right?"

"That's right," I confirm. "That's what her sister told me. She called Summer's testimony *a selfless sacrifice.*"

"Autumn's version of events doesn't match the information I have," Eric says. "According to my sources, Summer was a hostile witness."

"What does that mean?"

"It means her testimony was evasive. The prosecuting attorney alleged that Summer changed parts of her testimony from what she said in her original statement. Changes that would've helped the defendant."

"Are you saying Summer was reluctant to testify against the murder suspect?"

"That's what I'm saying," Eric replies. "According to my source, Summer wasn't an innocent bystander. She faced charges related to her involvement in the murder. The prosecutor believed Summer helped the killer dispose of the victim's body and gave the killer a fake alibi. If it weren't for the deal, Summer would have gone to prison."

"Deal?" I ask. "Why would the prosecution give her a deal if they believed she took part in a murder?"

"The prosecution needed Summer's testimony to convict the suspect. They wanted to prosecute him more than they wanted to prosecute Summer, so they offered her a deal. In exchange for her testimony, they granted Summer immunity, and because the prosecutor agreed that Summer's life would be at risk..." Eric's voice crackles and his words break up as the connection struggles to stay strong. "They offered..." more static and missing syllables. "...ness protec..." one last choppy sentence fragment, and the call ends.

I look at my phone. *No Service.*

"Shoot!" I grumble, stomping my foot.

The call failed before I could ask Eric the name of the killer Summer helped convict and the name of the victim.

What did he find out about Twyla?

With the clock ticking on Connie's fifteen-minute countdown, I emerge from the stairwell and knock on Billie's door.

"Oh, hey, Megan," says Billie, mid-yawn. She's wearing a long blue sleep shirt with the word, *Sleepyhead*, in cursive across the chest. Her eyes are heavy with sleep, and her mussed ginger hair looks like its last contact was with a pillow. "How are you?"

"I'm fine," I reply. "How are you? Autumn said you weren't feeling well this morning."

"I feel lousy," Billie admits. "But better than the first time I woke up." She runs her hands through her hair, taming her tousled tresses. "I'm glad you're here. I want to ask you something."

"Ask me anything." I smile.

"Yesterday, before Nadira showed up, you said you had experienced the same symptoms."

"I remember." I nod, recalling the weeks of exhausted nausea. "I felt awful."

"How long did it last?" Billie asks.

"Weeks," I reply. "Some days were worse than others."

"How did you make it stop?"

"It sorted itself out."

"Did you see a doctor?"

"Yup." I nod.

"What was the diagnosis?" Billie asks. "Was it a viral infection? What caused it?"

"Hannah."

"Hannah?" Comprehension sweeps across Billie's face. "Oh my," she gasps, gripping the door for support. "You were pregnant with Hannah?"

I nod.

"I'm not pregnant." Billie shakes her head. "I can't be pregnant." She laughs like it's the most absurd thing she's heard today. "Not yet." Billie's chest heaves with shallow breaths. "Can I?"

She does some mental math, counting on her fingers. "It's not part of the plan," she explains, her words quick and short as she paces back and forth in front of the open door. "We aren't scheduled to start trying until July," she exclaims. "It's only May." She combs her fingers through her hair. "We have a twelve-month plan. There's a spreadsheet." She throws her hands in the air. "Getting pregnant is in the July through December columns. Not the May column. A May pregnancy isn't on the schedule, Megan."

"Babies don't care about schedules."

I slide the pregnancy test out of my knitting bag. "Here." I hand Billie the box. "If you want to know for sure."

"Come in." Billie jerks her head toward the interior of the hotel room. "Can I take this anytime? Or do I have to wait until tomorrow morning?" she asks, reading the back of the box.

"I think you can take it anytime," I say. "But I haven't used one in years. You should do whatever the box says."

"I want to take it now," Billie says. "I need to know."

"Do you want to wait for Autumn?" I ask.

Billie sighs and drops her butt onto the bed.

"I don't want to pressure Autumn," she says. "She's dealing with too much already. It's unfair to ask her to deal with this too."

"She's your best friend," I say. "She might want to be here."

"I'm not sure about that," Billie says. "I feel like Autumn has been avoiding me since Summer died. When I'm in the room, she finds a reason to leave. When I join her at the spa, she finds an excuse to come back to the room." Billie looks at me with wide eyes. "What if Autumn is avoiding me because she thinks I killed Summer?"

"I'm sure she doesn't think that," I reassure her. "Do you think Autumn would continue to share a room with you if she believed you killed her sister?"

"I guess not," Billie agrees.

"Maybe Autumn just needs space to process her feelings."

"Will you stay while I do the test?"

"Sure," I reply, just as someone knocks on the door.

Billie gets up.

"I'll get it. It's Connie. I'm supposed to pack, and she's trying to keep me on task." I chuckle.

"While you talk to Connie, I'll pee on this stick."

"Are you OK, my dear?" Connie asks, craning her neck to look into the hotel room.

"I'm fine," I whisper. "But I need more time. Billie asked me to help her with something."

"Are you sure?" Connie asks. "You have that look in your eye. What are you up to?"

"I need to ask Billie some questions, but she's preoccupied."

"Her stomach issues?" Connie asks, rubbing her tummy in sympathy.

"Yes," I say. "She's in the bathroom right now."

"Fifteen more minutes," Connie says. "I'll be back in fifteen minutes if I don't see you packing in our room."

"Thank you."

I watch Connie return to our room across the hall and close the door.

"The box says the result takes three minutes," Billie says when she returns from the bathroom empty-handed. "I left the test on the edge of the tub so I won't check it every five seconds."

"Can I ask you something, Billie?" I ask, checking to proceed before I ask some personal questions about her relationship with Autumn and Summer.

"Sure," Billie says. "It'll help distract me for the next two minutes and fifty seconds."

"Why did you warn Autumn to be careful around Summer and be careful about trusting her?"

"Where did you hear that?"

"Someone mentioned it." I flick my wrist like I'm asking out of casual interest.

"It surprised me when Summer left witness protection and came home," Billie confides. "She had a fresh start where no one knew what she did, but she came back. I worried she had an agenda. I thought she came back for their mother's estate and would disappear again when she got it. Summer leaving again would have broken Autumn's heart."

Did Billie kill Summer to prevent her from breaking Autumn's heart?

"What do you mean, *no one knew what she did*?"

"Summer was a good person, for the most part," Billie explains. "But she made some poor decisions."

"For example?"

"Her choice of boyfriends, for a start," Billie replies. "Summer liked bad boys. She liked good-looking troublemakers. Complicated, rebellious guys."

"Was Summer's attraction to good-looking troublemakers the reason she witnessed a murder?"

"She didn't just witness the murder, she helped cover it up," Billie explains. "Summer's boyfriend committed the murder. She let him put the victim's body in her trunk. Then she drove the car to an abandoned lot where her boyfriend poured gas inside and set it on fire."

"That's not how Autumn explained it," I say. "She said Summer was an innocent bystander. She said the person Summer testified against was from an organized crime family, and his father threatened to kill Summer if she testified against his son."

"Except for the part about Summer being an innocent bystander, Autumn told you the truth," Billie confirms. "She didn't want you to judge Summer. Autumn believed that Summer's involvement in the murder case was an isolated incident."

"Do you believe it was an isolated incident?" I ask.

"I don't know." Billie shrugs. "We were so young when everything happened. We were barely adults. Who knows if Summer's involvement in the murder was a one-off or her first step toward a lifetime of bad choices? That's why I warned Autumn to be careful."

"Autumn must have believed it was one-off," I suggest. "Otherwise, she wouldn't have instructed her lawyer to transfer part ownership of the business to Summer."

"Autumn didn't transfer part ownership of the business to Summer," Billie insists.

"Yesterday, in the nail salon, Autumn told me she instructed her lawyer to transfer part ownership of the business to Summer. She said it would be a surprise."

"There's no way Autumn would do that without telling me," Billie scoffs. "I can prove it. I have access to her email."

Billie retrieves a laptop from the desk and cracks it open.

"You have access to Autumn's email?"

"Pretty much," Billie replies, typing in the password that unlocks the computer. "I know her computer password, which means I can access her email. Her lawyer would have wanted Autumn to make the request in writing. If she made the request, it'll be in her email. In the sent folder. I should be able to find it even without internet access."

I get the sense Billie has accessed Autumn's email before. She's too comfortable violating her best friend's online space for this to be the first time.

"Would Autumn be angry if she knew you checked her email?"

"Here!" Billie exclaims, ignoring my question. "Autumn emailed her lawyer on Friday before the storm hit." She beckons me to look at the laptop screen with her. "You're right," Billie utters, staring into the distance. "I can't believe it. But there it is." She blinks and looks at me with big, hurt eyes. "Why didn't Autumn tell me?"

"Maybe she didn't want you to worry," I reply. "May I read it?"

It's difficult to read the small font over Billie's shoulder.

"Sure." Billie hands me the laptop, then her phone dings. "The test!" She declares, silencing the alarm on her phone. "I forgot about the pregnancy test."

"Are you ready?" I ask.

"I think so."

"Do you want me to go with you?"

"No," Billie replies. "But can you wait here? Regardless of the result, I'm not sure how I'll feel about it."

"Take your time," I say. "You don't have to look at it this second."

Billie nods and swallows hard. She sits on the edge of the bed, grappling with the possibility that she's pregnant with a baby who doesn't care about schedules and spreadsheets.

Billie is right; the email's timestamp is a few hours before Friday's storm and Summer's murder. Could this email be part of Autumn's premeditated defence? Did she instruct her lawyer to transfer part of the family business to Summer so that, if the police accuse her of murdering her sister, Autumn can claim that if she was planning to kill her sister, she wouldn't have made her a business partner? Unless Autumn had second thoughts after she emailed her lawyer and killed Summer to stop the transfer. No, that doesn't make sense. Sending another email to her lawyer instructing him to cancel the transfer would be easier than committing murder.

Wait! What?

In the email's second paragraph, Autumn instructed her lawyer to change her will. According to the email, Billie is the sole beneficiary in Autumn's current will, but Autumn instructed her lawyer to add Summer as co-beneficiary, with each beneficiary inheriting fifty percent of Autumn's estate.

I bite my lips to hide my reaction.

Does Billie know about this? Should I ask her? I have a feeling she only read the first paragraph of the email, the part about transferring shares of the business from Autumn to Summer. The shock of Autumn not telling her about the business transaction and her potential pregnancy probably distracted her from reading the entire email.

I guess it makes sense Autumn named Billie as her beneficiary. When Summer was away, Billie was Autumn's closest friend. Her mother had died, and she had no one else to leave everything to. But Summer's return cuts Billie's future inheritance in half.

Jealousy wasn't Billie's only motive to kill Summer. Money and greed are excellent motives for murder too. Summer can't steal Billie's inheritance if she's dead. Does this mean Billie is planning to kill Autumn too? Am I alone in a hotel room with a murderer?

"Earth to Megan! Did you hear me?"

Billie's voice brings me back to the here and now.

"I'm sorry?"

I casually shield the laptop screen from Billie's view.

"I said, I'll be right back. I'm going to check the pregnancy test result."

"Good luck," I say. As soon as Billie turns her back, I snap a photo of the email with my cell phone, close Autumn's email, then close the laptop, and return it to the desk where Billie found it.

"One more question," I say as Billie approaches the bathroom door. "What was his last name? The guy whose family threatened to kill Summer if she testified."

"Clark," Billie replies as she disappears into the bathroom. "If you search the internet, you'll find lots of articles about the case."

Clark! The name makes my belly clench, but before I can contemplate my anxious response to Summer's ex-boyfriend's surname, Billie squeals.

"It's positive!" She skips out of the bathroom, waving the positive test in front of her and grinning from ear to ear. "I'm having a baby!" Billie throws her arms around my neck and bounces on the balls of her feet. "I'm not sick! I'm pregnant!"

"Happy Mother's Day."

CHAPTER 29

BILLIE'S CELEBRATORY bouncing comes to an abrupt halt when she slaps her hand over her mouth and runs to the bathroom to throw up.

Connie arrives for her next fifteen-minute check-in and, upon seeing Billie's ashen, shiny face, goes into mum-mode.

"Billie!" Connie swoops past me. "You need medical attention." She places a hand on Billie's clammy forehead. "I'm going down the hall to knock on the doctor's door."

"I'm pregnant!" Billie bursts. "See?" Grinning and with a slight bop, she holds up the test stick and gives it a triumphant wave. "But please don't tell anyone. I want to tell Autumn myself, and I don't want anyone else to find out until I tell my husband." She picks up her phone and rolls her eyes. "I'll phone him as soon as we get another wave of data connection."

"Congratulations!" Connie says, hugging Billie

around the shoulders. "What a wonderful story when you tell your future child how they made themselves known to you on Mother's Day!"

A subtle greenish tint washes across Billie's face and she gulps.

"Maybe you're right." Billie reaches for the ramekin of ginger lozenges that Nadira gave her yesterday, popping one in her mouth. "Maybe I should visit the doctor. Just to ask her a few questions."

Connie and I wait while Billie gets dressed, then walk her down the hall to the doctor's hotel room. The doctor is in, and she welcomes Billie into her room to talk and answer the expectant-mum's questions.

"Something happy came out of an unhappy weekend!" Connie claps her hands in front of her chest.

"So far," I say.

"So far, my dear?"

We take our time, dawdling toward our room, whispering with our heads together as I tell Connie about the email Autumn sent to her lawyer and, if Summer was still alive, how Billie's status would have changed from sole beneficiary to co-beneficiary.

"With Summer out of the way," Connie whispers, "not only would Billie get one-hundred percent of Autumn's estate, she would reclaim one-hundred percent of Autumn's time and attention."

"I hate the thought of Billie giving birth behind bars," I admit.

"Would you rather let a killer roam free?" Connie asks as we approach our door. "She can prowl around society"—Connie waves her limp hands with dramatic flair—"killing people willy-nilly because she doesn't want to share them with their siblings."

"We should knock on the connecting door and ask April, Tamara, and Rachel what they think about the fresh evidence against Billie."

"They aren't there, my dear," Connie advises. "They're on the hiking trails taking photos to post on social media."

The name and its significance hit me as soon as I grip the door handle.

"Clark!" I gasp, entering our hotel room.

"Who the heck is Clark?" asks Hannah, folding a sweatshirt and laying it in her suitcase.

"Clark is the lovely gentleman who washes windows on Water Street," Connie replies, then looks at me with her brow furrowed. "What does Clark have to do with anything?"

"Clark is the name of the family that threatened Summer for testifying," I explain. "It's also Maria's last name."

"Maria the spa manager?" Hannah asks.

I nod, lowering myself onto the bed and dropping my knitting bag to the floor.

"Let me get this straight," Hannah says, joining me on the bed and tucking her feet under her. "You think Summer testified against Maria's brother and helped convict him of murder?"

"It's possible." I nod. "I assumed it was her brother too, but maybe he was Maria's uncle or cousin."

"That's a pretty big leap, Mum," Hannah advises. "Just because they have the same last name doesn't mean Maria is related to the man Summer testified against."

"Hannah is right," Connie adds. "Clark is a common surname. Do we even know if Maria and the crime family share the same spelling? Some Clarks have an e at the end, some don't."

"Let's consider the evidence," I say, summoning my most cerebral voice. "Summer just returned from the witness protection plan." I raise my pinky finger. "She was in witness protection because the father of the man she testified against threatened to kill her."

I raise the finger next to it. "The family's last name is Clark." I raise a third finger. "Summer and Maria had at least two private, emotional conversations between Summer's arrival and her death. I can't confirm the details of those conversations because the only person who can corroborate is Summer, and she is dead."

I raise my index finger. "Maria's whereabouts during the blackout are unknown. This is also when someone lured the spa attendant away from the sauna, repositioned Summer's body, and stole the key."

I stick out my thumb and ball my other hand into a fist. "Before that, Maria had access to the smoothie ingredients because she worked at the juice bar before Nadira made Summer's Green Powerhouse smoothie."

I raise my pinky. "Also, Maria had access to spotted water hemlock. It grows right outside the perimeter of the spa gardens."

I raise my ring finger. "Even though Twyla hardly ever visits her at work, since Summer checked in, she drove up the mountain every day to visit Maria."

"If Maria is the killer, my dear, where does that leave Billie?" Connie asks, gesturing toward the door as if she expects Billie to appear there. "Five minutes ago, you gave me a list of evidence proving Billie murdered Summer."

"You have evidence that Billie killed Summer?" Hannah demands. "What evidence?"

"The Billie theory was *before* I made the Clark connection," I explain, looking at Connie. "The evidence against Maria makes a much more compelling case." I focus my attention on Hannah. "Just before Summer's murder, Autumn instructed her lawyer to transfer part of the family business into Summer's name and add Summer as co-beneficiary in her will."

"Co-beneficiary?" Hannah asks, picking up on the significance. "How many beneficiaries besides Summer?"

I hold up my index finger.

"Billie," I say.

Hannah makes a tiny *o* with her mouth and raises her eyebrows.

"Mum, the evidence against Billie is more compelling than the evidence against Maria."

"You're on Team Billie?" I ask.

"I wouldn't say *Team Billie*," Hannah objects. "It sounds like I'm cheering for her. That being said, in my opinion, based on the evidence you presented, Billie is the most likely suspect in Summer's murder."

Somewhere in Harmony Lake right now, Adam is grinning and puffing out his chest, unsure why he is suddenly bursting with pride.

"You sounded *exactly* like your father when you said that last sentence."

"You'll be a wonderful lawyer, Hannah!" Connie declares. "I can't wait to watch you in court."

"I'm on Team Maria," I say, bringing the conversation back to Summer's murder. "Hannah is on Team Billie. Connie, who do you think killed Summer?"

"Twyla."

"Twyla?" Hannah and I ask in stereo.

Given the events of the past hour, I'd forgotten Twyla was still in contention as Summer's killer.

"I think Twyla's motive was Maria," Connie suggests. "Imagine this." She clears her throat. "When Summer checked in, Maria recognized her as the witness whose testimony sealed the incarcerated-fate of her loved one. Powerful emotions consumed Maria. Anger." Connie makes an angry face. "Sadness." She frowns. "Hatred." Connie narrows her eyes until they're small slits and quirks her eyebrows.

"She confided in the person she trusts most in the world, Twyla. Maria told Twyla that she planned to exact revenge on her late-father's behalf and keep her family's promise to kill Summer. Twyla would never let Maria commit murder. She did it herself, convinced her police training meant she was clever enough to get away with it."

Connie waggles her index finger. "She planned to help investigate Summer's murder too. To position herself to manipulate any evidence that might point the finger of suspicion at herself or Maria. But she got stuck here when her patrol car floated away." She makes waves in the air with her hands. "Twyla arrived earlier than when Megan saw her walk in. She parked somewhere discreet, snuck the spotted water hemlock into the juice bar while the guests were having dinner, then snuck out using the dozens of back doors this place has. She dropped the baggie of spotted water hemlock on the deck chair when she made her escape, and either didn't notice, or couldn't risk coming back to search for it.

"Twyla lured the sauna attendant away from the saunas and met Maria there. Maria kept watch for the sauna attendant's return and ran interference with any guests who showed up while Twyla staged the crime scene. Twyla stole the key hoping it would delay the discovery of Summer's body and give her a vital piece of evidence should she need to frame someone else. Twyla planned to get far away from here before someone discovered Summer's body. Then, she could show up with her colleagues as if she hadn't been here at all."

"You're good," I acknowledge. "Whether your explanation is correct, they should make it into a movie."

"Question?" Hannah raises her hand, and Connie nods. "How did Twyla know to take the poison to the juice bar? I mean, how would she know to leave the spotted water hemlock at the juice bar? How would anyone know Summer would have a smoothie later? Twyla could have supplied the poison and delivered it, but someone else still had to add it to Summer's smoothie."

"Who?" I wonder out loud.

"The most obvious answer is Maria," Connie says. "She and Twyla are close. I'm sure they would trust each other with a massive secret. And Maria has a motive. It's unlikely they would have involved a third person. It's hard enough for two people to keep a secret, never mind three."

"Unless the third person was an unknowing accomplice," I suggest. "Nadira admitted she made Summer's smoothie. She wouldn't admit that if she had knowingly laced it with poison. Maybe, somehow, Maria knew Summer would have a smoothie. Summer had said she had a smoothie every day since she checked in," I suggest, grasping for a reasonable explanation for the killer's foresight.

"Nadira has been accused of poisoning a guest," Connie says, reminding me of the chicken-tofu scandal. "Maybe her involvement in Summer's murder isn't as farfetched as we think."

"Connie, may I borrow your phone?" Hannah asks.

"Of course, my lovely." Connie smiles and hands Hannah her phone.

Connie and I debate the suspects, their motives, their alibis, and opportunities.

After talking ourselves into circles, we conclude that while there's enough evidence to implicate each suspect, there's not enough evidence to eliminate anyone. We agree this is beyond our scope, and we've come as far as we can without the benefit of police resources and forensics.

"Are you sure it's safe?" Connie asks. "You can't confide in a murder suspect. What if Twyla killed Summer and comes unhinged because we've figured it out? Best-case scenario, she uses our intelligence to frame an innocent person for Summer's murder. Worst-case scenario, we end up on a sauna floor."

"She's the only law enforcement officer here," I plead. "Judging by the noise, the road crew will arrive any minute. When the road is clear, the killer will use it to get away with murder."

"What do you think, Hannah?" Connie asks.

Hannah's thumbs remind me of hummingbirds. They fly across the keyboard so fast, they're a blur hovering over the screen.

"Do you have service?" I ask, assuming she's typing a text.

"No." Hannah shakes her head without looking up or slowing down her thumbs. "I'm typing our theories into Connie's phone. If something happens to us, there's a written record of what we know." She stops typing and looks at Connie. "Don't give your phone to anyone. Next time we get a blip of service, the note will back up to the cloud. When it's backed up to the cloud, no one can destroy it, even if they destroy your phone."

"Whatever you say, my lovely." Connie smiles, taking the phone from Hannah.

"Mum, let's find Twyla."

As much as I admire my daughter's determination, I hesitate.

What if one of our theories is correct? What if we rattle the killer? They could panic and do something drastic. Summer's killer has nothing to lose and is growing more desperate by the minute.

The road crew won't be alone when they get here. Police cars, the coroner, and a forensics team will be right behind them.

"We have to stay with Connie," I say. "We agreed to stay together until we're safe from Summer's killer or get away from this mountain."

"I'll be fine," Connie insists. "I'll finish packing our things. I promise to lock the door and not open it for anyone." She gestures to the connecting door between the adjoining rooms. "I'll lock the connecting door too." She flicks her wrist. "Besides, the Shaws will be here any minute. They still have to pack."

Phone in hand, Hannah wraps her hand around the doorknob and looks at me.

"Well?"

Connie gives me an encouraging nod.

"Fine," I concede with a sigh and an anxious knot swelling in my stomach. "Let's go."

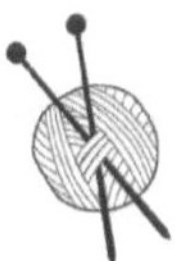

CHAPTER 30

THE LOBBY IS a hub of activity. Both massage chairs are occupied, and groups of chatty guests dot the sofas and chairs. There are two people ahead of me at the front desk.

"Hi," I say, when the desk attendant summons me with a smile. "Do you know where Twyla is?"

"No," she replies, shaking her head. "I haven't seen her this morning." She picks up the two-way radio in front of her. "I'll hunt her down for you. It might take a few minutes to locate her."

"Thank you," I respond.

"I'll broadcast a message." She fidgets with the dials. "If someone is near Twyla, they'll tell me where she is."

"Thanks," I say again. "In the meantime, I'll loiter around the massage chairs, waiting for a turn." I smile and turn to walk away.

"Samosas," Nadira sings, blocking my path with the food cart she's pushing. "I'm trying out some new variations." She brings the cart to a stop. "I'd love every-one's opinion!" Nadira pinches the centre of an unfolded cloth napkin and snaps her wrist, flicking the napkin off the food cart to reveal a platter of samosas.

"Curry vegetable." She flicks another cloth napkin. "Spicy pork." With extra flourish, Nadira flicks the third cloth napkin and reveals the third steamy platter. "And last but not least, beef." She smiles.

A table top sign with the flavour handwritten in red ink pokes through the centre of each platter.

The samosas tease me with their appetizing aroma. I'm tempted but refuse to let the yummy, fresh, steamy food distract me from my mission to find Twyla.

"Would you like a samosa, Megan?" asks Nadira.

"No thank you," I smile. "I'm still full from the wonderful breakfast you made."

I want to tell Nadira that Billie's tummy troubles had nothing to do with the food at the spa but resist the urge for fear that I might divulge Billie's secret.

Scanning the crowded lobby for Hannah, I catch my daughter settling into a massage chair. The other chair is still occupied.

"The lady at the desk is trying to track down Twyla," I say. "I'm going to the gift shop to pick up some soaps and lotions."

"OK," Hannah says, futzing with the massage settings.

"Do you want anything?"

"No, thank you." She rests the back of her head on the chair and closes her eyes.

"Megan!"

I stop in the gift shop doorway and snap my head left then right, searching for the source of my name.

"Over here," Maria says, smiling and waving as she comes toward me. "Hi."

"Hi, Maria."

"I hear you're looking for Twyla."

"That's right," I say. "Do you know where she is?"

"She's helping an injured hiker," Maria explains. "April's daughter…" Maria hesitates, searching for her name.

"Rachel," I say, filling in the blank. "Are my friends OK?"

"Your friends are fine," Maria assures me.

"Good."

I sigh with relief.

"Rachel ran back alone about fifteen minutes ago. She and her parents found an injured guest on the hiking trail. They think she broke her ankle. April and Tamara stayed with the hiker, and Rachel ran back for help. She's leading Twyla to the hiker's location."

"It sounds like Twyla won't get back for a while," I comment.

"I'm glad I bumped into you." Maria looks around, assessing the crowded lobby. "Can we talk?" She inches closer to me. "In private? We can talk in my office."

"OK," I reply. "I'll meet you there in two minutes."

Maria steps behind the front desk, helping herself to a few samosas on the way, and I lure a reluctant Hannah away from the massage chair.

"Come in," Maria calls when I knock on her office door.

"Hi," I say.

"Hi," Hannah says, following me into the small office.

"Hannah!" Maria widens her eyes and blinks like Hannah might be an illusion. "I didn't know you were joining us."

"Here I am!" Hannah chuckles and makes jazz hands, once again reminding me that she is her father's personality in a twenty-year-old woman's body.

"What do you want to talk about?" I ask.

"The *thing* I gave you earlier."

Maria says, *thing* like I should know its hidden meaning.

"Thing?" I ask, feigning ignorance, but knowing she's inquiring about the pregnancy test she gave me.

"You know. *The THING.*" Maria draws out the last word and nods slowly. "The thing you asked me for."

"What thing?" Hannah asks.

"Right," I say. "I remember. What about it?"

"I'm just following up to make sure it worked, and you're happy with the result."

She's following up because she's nosy. She wants to know if I used the test and what the result was.

"Worked?" Hannah asks. "What did she give you?"

I squeeze Hannah's hand to acknowledge her question and let her know we'll talk about it later.

"It worked as expected." I smile. "Thank you for your concern."

"You used it?" Maria confirms.

"It was used, yes." I nod.

"If you want to talk about it, I'm here." Maria smiles and squeezes her shoulders toward her ears. "I'm a superb listener," she adds.

"I'll keep your offer in my back pocket in case I need it," I say. "Can I ask you something?"

"Anything!" Maria sits up straight, giving me her full attention.

"Why did Twyla park so far from the spa on Friday during the storm?"

"Who said she parked far from the spa?" Maria asks, answering my question with a question.

"She must have," I reply, thinking back to Connie's detailed theory about Summer's murder. "The storm washed away the road below us but the parking lot was undamaged. The storm could only have washed away Twyla's car if she had parked at least a quarter-mile down the road."

"You're right," Maria admits. "Twyla parked down the road. Like she always does."

"Why?" I ask.

"I asked her to," Maria explains. "Whenever Twyla visits me at work while she's on duty, her patrol car draws attention and distracts guests. When they see a police car, guests assume something bad happened. They get anxious and ask why the police are here. When I tell them the police aren't here on official business, they think I'm lying. Guests who didn't see the car, hear about it, and next thing I know, rumours and speculation are rampant. SoulSpring Spa and Retreat is a haven for relaxation and rejuvenation, not an epicentre for stress and speculation."

"She must love you a lot to walk a quarter-mile up the road during a violent spring storm."

Maria smiles.

"Your last name is Clark?" Hannah asks, pointing to the nameplate on Maria's desk.

"That's right."

"Are you related to the organized crime family with the same name?"

If Hannah is using the element of surprise to gauge Maria's reaction, goal achieved. Maria's eyes widen. She pulls herself to her full-seated height and clears her throat.

"Clark is a popular surname." Maria smiles.

"Was the man who went to prison your brother?" Hannah asks. "Mum and I assumed he was your brother. Then we realized he might be your cousin or uncle."

"You know," Maria says, acknowledging the truth.

"We suspect," I say. "Are we right?"

"Yes," Maria confirms. "Summer was my brother's girlfriend. She testified against him, and he went to prison for murder. He passed away late last year from a brain aneurysm. He died alone on the cold cement floor of his cell. A guard found him."

Maria's brother died on the floor of a locked cell. Summer died on the floor of a locked sauna. Coincidence or calculated revenge?

"I'm sorry for your loss," I say.

"Sorry," Hannah says.

"Listen," Maria pleads, spreading her fingers on the desk. "No one else at the spa knows I'm a Clark." She stumbles over her words and takes a breath, then blows it out. "I mean, they know my last name is Clark, but they don't know my father orchestrated international art heists and brokered black-market deals for priceless, smuggled artifacts. Or that my brother worked for him and took care of their less glamorous, more violent tasks."

"They won't find out from us," I assure her.

"Does Twyla know about your family?" Hannah asks.

"Of course," Maria replies. "We grew up in the same town. We're younger than them, but Twyla and I went to school with Billie and the twins."

"Did you tell Twyla that Summer was staying here?"

Maria nods. "Twy worried that seeing Summer was too much for me. She thought I might have a breakdown. I lost my father and brother within a few months of each other. They both died unexpectedly, and their deaths hit me hard. Summer walking into the spa on Wednesday shocked me. I'm sure when I called Twy to tell her, I sounded unstable."

"That's why Twyla visited you every day," I say. "Not because you were helping with her resume or because they dispatched her during the storm. She was worried about you."

Maria nods. "I recognized Summer the moment I

laid eyes on her. The reservation was in Billie's married name. I didn't know Billie's married name and didn't realize she was the same Billie who was best friends with Autumn and Summer. The last person I expected to see was Summer. When the twins walked in, my heart pounded, and I couldn't breathe. I got someone else to serve them. I lied about an emergency in the mud baths. Then I locked myself in my office and phoned Twyla."

"Did Summer recognize you?"

"Yes." Maria nods. "We both look different now. We're older. My hair is longer, Summer's was shorter, but we recognized each other. She hid the shock better than me, but I saw the recognition in her eyes. I knew Summer better than I knew Autumn because Summer used to hang out at my house with my brother."

"You could tell the twins apart?" I ask.

"Always," Maria says. "They had identical features, similar taste in clothes, and even wore their hair the same, but there were subtle differences. Autumn is uptight. She walks fast, is socially awkward, and she smiles like she saw it in a movie once but isn't sure she's doing right. She's a typical type-A personality. Autumn is a good person, and she has kind eyes.

"Summer was laid back, chronically late, and had horrible posture. She loved small talk and got bored easily. Her smile was a lopsided grin. Like she knew something but wouldn't tell you. Her eyes appeared kind, but if you watched long enough, you'd get a glimpse of the dark, soulless place behind them. I could always tell Summer and Autumn apart."

I believe her. If Maria dislikes Summer, there isn't a hint of anger or contempt in her voice or her demeanour. She's just stating the facts as she knows them.

"What did you and Summer talk about during those huddled, emotional conversations?" I ask.

"Hours after they checked in, Summer came looking for me," Maria explains. "I was still in shock after seeing her earlier that day. I had hoped we could avoid each other for the duration of her stay, but she insisted that we talk."

"About what?"

"She wanted me to know that they didn't know I worked here when they booked their stay. Summer said she didn't want to upset me. She offered to leave if I wanted her to."

"Did you want her to?" I ask.

"Yes," Maria replies. "But I told Summer that she, Autumn, and Billie were welcome guests. She also told me she had heard about my brother and father. She gave me her condolences. Summer said she was sorry about everything that happened between her and my brother. She tried to justify her decision to take the deal and testify against him. She asked for my forgiveness and tried to convince me she was a different person now."

"Did you forgive her?" Hannah asks.

"I forgave Summer a long time ago," Maria replies.

"Forgiveness is for the forgiver, not the forgiven. I didn't want to live the rest of my life tethered to my past by anger."

"Did you believe Summer when she told you she was a different person?" I ask.

"No," Maria replies without hesitation. "When I opened my mouth to tell her I forgave her, I saw something familiar in her eyes. Her voice and the rest of her face matched her repentant words, but Summer's eyes were empty. Not a hint of genuine emotion. I couldn't say the words. Instead, I burst into tears and excused myself from the conversation."

"Was that your last conversation with Summer?"

"No." Maria shakes her head. "After our first conversation, I journaled about my feelings. I meditated on the situation and realized I didn't want to be Summer's excuse for not living up to her potential. I didn't want her to use my lack of forgiveness to justify falling back into her old ways."

"That's a very mature and insightful attitude," I comment.

"On Friday morning, while most guests were having breakfast, I encountered Summer alone in the lobby. It was a message from the universe. I approached her, forgave her, and wished her well. I told her I hoped she lives her best life."

"What did Summer say?"

"She thanked me. She said my forgiveness meant a lot to her. Then she asked me something kind of odd and off-topic."

"What did Summer ask you?"

"She pointed out that I had approached her and forgiven her without making sure I was talking to the right twin. She asked how I could always tell her apart from Autumn," Maria says with a chuckle. "Summer said I was the only person the twins could never fool. She said they could even fool their mother if they set their minds to it. It amazed her that after all these years, I could still tell them apart."

The timing is odd. But if I had a twin, and only one person could tell us apart, I'd want to know how they do it.

"What did you say?" Hannah asks.

"The same thing I told you." Maria shrugs one shoulder. "Except the part about Autumn having kind eyes and Summer's eyes being void of emotion. I left that out for obvious reasons." Maria clears her throat. "Now that I've answered your questions and bared my soul, I'd like you to answer a question for me."

"Shoot," I say.

"It's about *the thing*," Maria says. "What was the outcome?"

I can't believe she's still thinking about the pregnancy test.

"Positive," I say with a wink.

"Are we happy or sad?"

"Happy."

CHAPTER 31

"Do you still think Maria killed Summer?" Hannah whispers as we linger within sight of the massage chairs, hoping they'll become available before Twyla returns from her rescue mission.

"We can't eliminate her," I reply. "Maria had motive, and she had opportunity. She also had access to spotted water hemlock and Summer's smoothie ingredients. Summer checked in on Wednesday morning, giving Maria two days to plan the murder."

"But Maria is spiritual and grounded. She's at peace with her family's past. She wouldn't kill anyone in case Karma punished her for it."

"I know what you mean," I admit. "But maybe she acts more at peace than she is. Maybe she's serene and Zen because she killed Summer and justifies it because the universe sent her a sign or something."

"Mine!" Hannah blurts, then jumps into the massage chair when the current occupant vacates it.

"I'm going to the gift shop again," I say.

"I'll be here," Hannah says, her voice wobbling from the vibration of the mechanical massage hands.

———

"HI, MEGAN."

"Hi, Billie." I turn to face her without disturbing the precarious pile in my arms. "How are you feeling?"

"Not bad," she replies. "The sickness is more bearable now that I know why it's happening." Billie points in front of me. "It's your turn."

"Is that all you're buying?" I ask, pointing my chin at the bottle of ginger ale she holds in one hand and the sports drink she holds in the other.

"Yeah," she says. "Doctor's orders. She said the sports drink will help replace some electrolytes." She holds up the other bottle. "And my mother always gave me ginger ale when I had an upset tummy."

"Go ahead of me," I insist, stepping aside. "It'll take forever for me to cash out. You only have two items."

"Thanks."

Billie smiles and steps up to the counter.

"How was your visit with the doctor?" I ask.

"It was good," Billie replies. "She said nausea is a normal pregnancy symptom. But she wants me to see a doctor tomorrow. She said there's a chance I might have hyperemesis gravidarum, and my doctor will want to monitor me."

"Is that as serious as it sounds?"

"It's the medical name for relentless nausea," Billie explains, "Anyway, Twyla cut our conversation short when she banged on the door. She needed the doctor's help with an injured hiker or something."

Between Summer's death, Billie's pregnancy, and an injured hiker, the doctor's spa weekend is more like a business trip than a relaxing getaway. I know how she must feel. If I wanted to find a dead body, I would've stayed home. Goodness knows, I've found more than my share in Harmony Lake.

"Speaking of Twyla," I say. "Is it true that you grew up with Twyla and Maria?"

"Yes," Billie says, paying the cashier for her purchase. "We didn't hang out with Maria and Twyla, but we knew each other." She smiles and takes the small bag from the cashier. "I'll see you later, Megan. I'm going upstairs to pack, then lie down for a while."

I unload my armful of artisanal soaps, travel-size organic lotions, and scented candles on to the counter.

"Did you find everything you were looking for?" asks the sales clerk as she organizes my self-care haul and returns the toppled bottles to their upright positions.

"Yes." I smile. "Thank you."

The clerk is about to scan my first item when her face lights up.

"Are those the samosas everyone is talking about?" asks the eager cashier as she slides my items aside and leans across the counter.

"A fresh batch!" Nadira rolls up with her food cart,

stopping next to me. Again. I swear these samosas are conspiring to force me to eat them.

The scrumptious samosa aroma, and Nadira's repeat performance of her dramatic three-platter reveal, attracts a crowd of spa guests and employees.

Not being someone who would come between hungry people and a fresh batch of gourmet samosas, I pluck one from the vegetable curry platter and step away from the counter.

"I'll browse the mud masks until you're ready."

The cashier nods and gives me a thumbs-up because her mouth is full.

Moments later, I'm wishing I'd grabbed two samosas and comparing the ingredients of a kaolin clay mask against the ingredients of a red clay mask.

Movement in the corner of my eye distracts me from the labels. Autumn slips into the gift shop and takes a bottle of water from the refrigerator. The hood is up on her unseasonable, fluffy, fleece, hooded sweatshirt. She makes her way to the shelves of snack food near the counter. She picks up a pack of sugar-free gum and a bag of nuts as she inches closer to the food cart and infiltrates the crowd of enthusiastic snackers around the samosa platters.

A drip of excitement tickles my belly, and I'm struck by a sense of captivated awe. The same feeling I get when I'm sitting in the backyard, minding my business, and a squirrel or bird approaches me, suspending its fear of humans and granting us a rare, close-up encounter with each other.

I stay so still I even hold my breath in case an exhale spooks Autumn and she takes off.

I'm not proud of watching someone who doesn't know they're being watched, but I can't make myself look away. I bend my knees slightly to reduce the amount of me that's visible above the shelf. Is this what stalkers do? Am I stalking Autumn? Why am I so intrigued by her?

Autumn squeezes her way to the front of the crowd. She assesses the platters of samosas. She arranges the water bottle, nuts, and gum so they're in the same hand. Then, with her free hand, Autumn reaches for the first platter, vegetable curry samosas. She reads the sign and retracts her hand, moving it to the next platter. In one quick motion, Autumn takes a samosa from the spicy chicken platter and a second samosa from the beef platter. Who are they for? They can't be for Autumn because she's a pescatarian. A loud, dedicated pescatarian.

Clutching the samosas in her hand, Autumn backs out of the crowd and retreats to the magazine racks where I can't see her.

I return the clay masks to the shelf and creep through the store toward the magazine racks.

Autumn is chewing fast. Her eyes dart this way and that, furtively checking her surroundings. Just as she raises the second triangle pastry to her mouth and bites into it, our eyes meet.

"Megan," Autumn mumbles with her mouth full.

I gasp and stare into her wide, empty eyes.

I rush out of the gift shop with one thing on my mind.

"Hannah!" I grab her forearm and yank her out of the massage chair.

"I have to turn it off." She reaches for the chair's controller, but we're already out of arm's reach. "Mum, I should reset it for the next person."

"No time," I say, pulling her along behind me like a defiant toddler.

"Where are we going?"

"Upstairs," I say. "We're locking ourselves in our room until help gets here."

"What happened?" Hannah jerks her arm from my grasp and stops. "Why are we rushing?"

"I saw her," I say. "And she knows I saw her. We're not safe."

I grab Hannah's hand and tug my reluctant daughter toward the stairwell.

"Who did you see?" She stops again, reclaims her hand, and crosses her arms in front of her chest.

Why does she have to choose now to ask questions? Why did she have to get too big to carry? Why won't she let me drag her to safety?

"Sweetie." I summon my most composed and rational voice. "I know who the killer is. I know why she did it. She knows I know. She's unstable and psychotic and has nothing to lose. We aren't safe. She'll do anything to keep her secret. I need you to cooperate." I take a calming breath to maintain my composed and rational facade. "Now, please let me take you upstairs and lock you in our hotel room," I say, sounding far less composed and much more irrational than I intend.

Hannah squints. An unsuccessful attempt to conceal the confusion and concern in her eyes as she considers my words.

"Twyla and the Shaws are miles away helping an injured hiker, which means Connie is all alone," I say, hoping to appeal to my daughter's affection for Connie.

Hannah nods, lurches past me, and opens the stairwell door.

"Who killed Summer?" she asks as I rush past her.

"It's not that easy," I say, leaning against the closed door so *she* can't follow us. "Nothing is how it seems."

"You're not making sense, Mum."

"I'll explain everything as soon as we're safe."

"Connie!" Hannah declares, remembering why she agreed to listen to me.

She grabs the handrail and conquers the first flight of stairs two-at-a-time, disappearing around the corner before I start my ascent. The thumping of her feet bounding up the stairs is the only evidence Hannah is still ahead of me.

"Hannah!" I shout, more breathless than I care to admit. "Wait!" I stop on the landing between the first and second floors. "Hannah?"

I tilt my ear into the silence, forcing myself to tune out the heartbeat pounding in my ears and listen for the thumping of Hannah's feet. Nothing. She must have stopped on the second-floor landing.

"Mu—"

Who muffled her voice?

"Hannah?"

A rush of adrenaline cures my breathlessness. I launch myself to the third step and take the rest of the stairs two at a time. Each leap reveals a bit more of the second-floor landing. As I search every new inch of the landing for a sign of Hannah, she slides into view. The backs of her hands are against her shoulders and her eyes are wide. She is trembling.

She is terrified.

Hannah gives me an almost indiscernible head shake.

A silent warning to stay back.

"Why?" I demand. "What's wrong?"

Hannah shuffles sideways, and the trigger of her fear comes into view. Someone is pressing a gun into my daughter's back.

CHAPTER 32

"How did you find us?" I freeze on the spot, looking up at them from the second last step.

I control my breathing, taking measured breaths, and forcing my heaving lungs into submission.

I can't let her see my fear.

I've never been more afraid in my life.

"When you and your daughter stopped to have a pair of hissy fits in the lobby, I snuck past you and ran up the stairs." She grins. "I knew you'd take the stairs. You *always* take the stairs." She scoffs. "You're not the only one who's observant, you know."

"Well done."

Despite my sarcastic tone, she interprets it as a genuine compliment and smiles. I want to punch the arrogant, lop-sided smile off her stupid, smug face.

"You should have seen yourself. You looked like you saw a ghost." She laughs.

"I kind of did," I point out.

"Was it the samosas?" she asks. "Is that how you figured out it was me?"

I shake my head.

"It was the eyes."

"I was sure it was the samosas." She sighs. "If I never see another piece of fish again, it'll be too soon." She chuckles. "The samosas were a lazy mistake, but I was desperate for something meaty. Getting away with eating the lamb chop made me overconfident."

"The lamb chop you ate after you planted the missing sauna key in Billie's luggage?"

Summer nods.

"Twyla was asking too many questions," she explains. "I think she was starting to suspect something. She visited our room yesterday and spent too long searching our belongings. Then she came back today before breakfast and searched again. I'm sure she thinks I killed my sister."

"Summer, please let Hannah go," I plead. "I'll switch places with her. You can hold the gun against my back."

She grimaces. "It's still strange to hear my name," she says, ignoring my plea. "I just can't get used to it. I got used to my witness protection name, and Autumn's name, right away." She shakes her head. "But my name doesn't sound like it belongs to me anymore."

Summer clears her throat.

Hannah flinches.

Summer panics and raises the barrel of the gun from

between Hannah's shoulder blades to the back of her head.

Hannah whimpers.

"It's OK, sweetie!" I move my foot to the last step before the landing, bringing me within arm's reach of them. I reach toward Hannah but don't allow myself to touch her. "It's OK. Shhhh."

I settle for muttering comforting *shhh* sounds instead of telling Hannah: stay calm. We can't freak out Summer. We can't fluster her. Let's keep her relaxed. Distract her while we figure out how to get away.

"Why do you have a gun?" I ask, wondering why she killed her sister with a toxic plant when she clearly has a gun.

"The gun was Plan B," Summer replies. "In hindsight, Plan B would've been easier."

"What was plan A?" I ask.

"Plan A was for my sister to die in her sleep. It was supposed to look like she died of something undiagnosed."

"Why did you choose spotted water hemlock?" I ask.

"It's less obvious than a gunshot wound. It would've been impossible for the police to declare my sister died of natural causes if there was a bullet in her. Spotted water hemlock grows everywhere around here," Summer explains. "If the police discovered she had died from ingesting spotted water hemlock, I would've convinced them she confused it with parsley or some other herb. They would have believed me because I'm Autumn now. Everyone believes Autumn. Autumn doesn't lie. Autumn is a good person, She's an honest, productive, and respected member of society. She has no criminal record."

"You added the spotted water hemlock to your own smoothie, then when Autumn wasn't looking, you switched smoothies with her?"

"Yes." Summer nods. "Only a small amount. It only takes a small amount. I didn't mix it in very much, so the dark green leaf pieces weren't visible through the cup." She squints at me. "How did you know it was spotted water hemlock?"

"We found your baggie," I reply. "It fell out of your bag when you bumped into the doctor."

"I didn't realize I'd lost it until I went looking for it." Summer shakes her head. "I figured it fell out on the deck. I had breakfast there this morning so I could look for it. After Autumn died, I made sure to put her finger-prints all over the bag so the police would believe that she added it to her smoothie herself."

"Why did you try to frame Billie?" I ask.

"I always planned to pin it on Billie if the police discovered Autumn was murdered and wouldn't believe my parsley story."

"That's why you planted the key in her luggage?"
Summer nods.

"You said Autumn was supposed to die in her sleep, but she died in the sauna," I point out.

"Between fifteen minutes and three hours is a big window of time, Megan," Summer explains, rolling her eyes and prolonging the *n* in my name. "Autumn decided she wanted a smoothie *before* the sauna instead of *after*. I knew it was my last chance of the day to poison her. She wouldn't have ingested anything else until the next morning."

"Why did you steal her identity?"

The irony! Summer left the new identity and new life she'd built in witness protection, so she could reclaim her old identity and old life, then killed her sister to assume her identity.

"I killed her to reclaim my life," Summer clarifies. "While I lived a made-up life as a made-up person, Autumn lived my life. The life that should have been mine. The life I wanted. I wanted to live in our hometown with our friends and family. I wanted to learn the family business so I could take over one day. I wanted to take care of my sick mother. I wanted to go to her funeral. No one understands I gave up everything when I went into witness protection, then I gave up everything again to come back."

Ten years ago, she became a different person to avoid a prison sentence for her role in killing someone, and now she'll serve a prison sentence for killing someone to become a different person. The prison psychiatrist will have a field day untangling this.

"But you came back," I say. "Most people in witness protection never see their loved ones again. You got a second chance to be Summer."

"No, I didn't," Summer insists through gritted teeth. "No one gave me a second chance. I gave up a secure future with guaranteed income, and everyone treated me like a criminal. I'm tired of being defined by one unfortunate decision I made over a dozen years ago."

Now she'll be defined for two unfortunate decisions.

"Maybe people just need more time," I suggest, hoping sympathy will keep her talking and keep my daughter alive until help arrives. "Maybe they're scared you'll leave again."

"My sister wouldn't give me a job or my fair share of our mother's estate," she hisses.

"But she did, Summer," I say, attempting to make her less agitated. "Autumn instructed her lawyer to add you to her will and to transfer part of the family business to you. I read the email."

"It was me, Megan." Summer shakes her head and clucks her tongue, pitying my gullibility. "I sent the email. I sent it before I killed Autumn. It was risky to leave it in her sent folder. She could've found it by accident. But I needed to ensure the police would find it if necessary. The email was part of my plan to frame Billie."

"Of course, it was," I say with a sigh. "You're clever. You lured the sauna attendant away from her desk while you staged Autumn's body and stole the key, and before you went public with your sister's assumed identity, you tested your Autumn impersonation on Maria, the only person who could always tell you apart. That's why you visited the front desk on Friday night. You didn't ask Maria for pain killers because you had a headache, you were testing her to make sure you could pass as Autumn. After you passed the test, you put the second part of your plan into action, delaying the discovery of Autumn's body as long as possible."

"Nice deduction, Miss Marple." Summer sneers. "If there's one thing I learned in witness protection, it was how to lie. My whole life was a lie. I practiced being Autumn for weeks. Her walk, her bossy voice, her tense smile, and her rigid posture. It's not as easy as you'd think." Summer shakes her head. "We might look identical, but I'm nothing like my sister."

"How did you know the sauna attendant would believe you when you lied about her boyfriend cheating in a massage room?"

"It's called paying attention, Megan. You should try it." Summer's words ooze smugness. "I listen to conversations around me. Autumn loved the sauna. We were there every day. The sauna worker was always on the phone. She went on and on about her suspicions that her boyfriend was doing the nasty with a massage therapist called Logan."

"I'm surprised Billie didn't figure out you were Summer pretending to be Autumn," I say, bringing us back to her sister's murder.

"If she wasn't so distracted by puking and sleeping, she would have," Summer says.

"That's why you've avoided her since you killed your sister," I theorize. "We thought you were in shock, but you were avoiding detection."

"I was planning to end Autumn and Billie's friendship," Summer confesses. "Otherwise, it was only a matter of time before Billie realized something wasn't right with Autumn and started putting it together."

"You've thought of everything," I commend her.

"Don't be glib," Summer says, shifting her weight from foot-to-foot with increasing frequency. "You think you're better than me, but you're not. We're the same except you got away with your bad decisions. Everybody is bad, Megan. Some people, like you, believe they're good because they don't get caught."

"I'm not better than you," I say. "I'm not a good person or a bad person. Neither are you. There's an entire spectrum between good and bad, Summer, and most of us fall somewhere in the middle."

"Why does everything you say sound so preachy?" She rolls her eyes. I assume her question is rhetorical. "Self-righteous people like you need bad people like me. I give you someone to feel superior to."

"Just because you've made a bad decision, or two, doesn't mean you're a bad person."

Summer uses the back of her gun-holding hand to wipe beads of sweat from her brow.

I give Hannah a reassuring nod and a small smile. She returns the tiniest nod.

"I am a bad person," Summer says. "I killed my sister. Before that, I stood by and watched someone else get murdered. Then I helped dispose of their body. I'm the bad twin. Autumn was the good twin. And look where that got her…"

A cough echoes through the stairwell, interrupting

Summer's disturbing rant. We all look up at the ceiling, certain the sound originated from above us.

Is someone on the next landing? Who? How much did they hear? If they come down here, will Summer kill them? Will she kill Hannah?

I need a plan. Now.

"The gun isn't loaded."

Twyla?

"One step closer and I'll shoot the girl," Summer threatens.

I release the handrail, my fingers and knuckles stiff from the death grip I had on it. I shake my hands and wipe my sweaty palms on my thighs, leaving a dark streak on the thighs of my yoga pants.

"With what?" Twyla asks. "The gun is empty. I found it tucked into a secret compartment in Summer's suitcase when I searched your room. I took the ammo. All of it. There are no bullets in that gun."

"You're lying," Summer exclaims, moving the gun away from Hannah and pointing it up the stairs toward the landing between the second and third floors. She looks at me. "Twyla's lying."

Summer inspects the gun like she just caught it lying to her.

A bead of sweat streams down the side of Summer's forehead and past her temple.

Hannah glares at me, recalibrating her attitude and her body. She balls her hand into a fist and narrows her gaze on me. Her jaw clenches and unclenches. She bends her arm and cocks her elbow, raising her shoulder. Her forearm is rigid and tense.

Lucky for us, her bullet situation distracts Summer, and she doesn't notice the subtle changes to Hannah's posture.

Sensing that Hannah has a plan and is waiting for the right moment to execute it, I stealthily switch feet so my dominant, right foot is on the step above me, and grip the handrail with my less dominant, left hand. I'm prepared to launch myself, if necessary, and my dominant hand is free to help Hannah with whatever she plans to do.

A loud clink reverberates through the stairwell. Metal hitting concrete. A bullet dropping to the floor above us.

"That wasn't a bullet," Summer shouts, glowering at me. "She dropped a key or a coin. She's trying to psych me out." Summer nods fast and swallows. "This gun is loaded." She shakes the butt of the gun. "I loaded it myself. If you don't believe me, I'll shoot your daughter to prove it."

"You can't shoot anyone with an empty gun, Summer," Twyla says. "Do yourself a favour and give up. You're surrounded and outnumbered."

Twyla used Summer's name. She knows who Summer is. Had she already figured it out, or was she standing there throughout Summer's confession?

"Shut up!" Summer screeches, stretching her arm to aim the gun up the stairs.

This is the farthest the gun has been from Hannah's body since Summer took her hostage.

This is our opportunity.

I nod at Hannah.

She nods back.

"Now!" Hannah shouts, scrunching her face and ramming her elbow into Summer's stomach and ribs.

The blow takes Summer by surprise. Winded and knocked off balance, she collapses at the waist, bending forward as she draws her arms protectively toward her torso.

Hannah grabs Summer's wrist and squeezes, digging her fingertips into the tendons and ligaments below Summer's palm.

Summer howls in agony, fighting the involuntary loosening of her grip on the gun. Her hand opens, her fingers contorted with pain and resistance.

The gun lands on the floor with a resounding clamour.

I launch myself toward the landing, gripping the handrail for balance, squeeze my hand around Summer's forearm and wrench her toward me as hard as I can, letting out a loud grunt.

Summer tumbles down the stairs, and I use the handrail to pull myself out of her way.

I leap to the landing and push Hannah against the wall, trapping her behind me where she is safe.

I'm a panting, sweaty mess.

Summer's gun is on the floor only feet away from

me. Calling me. It would take less than one second to grab it.

Summer's crumpled body lies on the landing at the bottom of the stairs. Her eyelids flutter, and she moans.

My eyes flit back and forth between Summer and the gun. The gun she insisted has bullets in it.

Thirteen steps separate me from Summer. A clear shot.

The ball of rage and fear roiling in my gut pull me toward the gun like a magnet.

I want to do it so bad.

Summer could never hurt my daughter again. She could never hurt anyone. Ever. The world would be safer.

I could say I grabbed the gun to secure it, and it went off by accident. Oops! How did that happen? I've never used a gun; I didn't know what I was doing. My hands were sweaty and shaky. My finger must have slipped.

I want to destroy the person who threatened my daughter's life. But I refuse to take a step forward and leave Hannah unprotected.

"Mum." She taps my shoulder. "I can't breathe." She gasps. "Stop backing up." She wheezes. "You're squeezing me against the wall."

I take a half-step forward. Closer to the gun.

"Sorry," I say without taking my eyes off Summer or the gun.

Hannah takes a deep breath against my back.

Momentum surges through my body, and with my gaze fixed on the gun, my body twitches.

Just as I lunge, the clomping of boots diminishes my lunge to a dramatic wince. Twyla lands with a thud in front of me. She secures the gun, taking the choice out of my hands.

"Everyone all right?" Twyla asks, scanning Hannah and I from head to toe.

"Yes."

"Uh-huh."

Hannah and I nod.

"You did good," Twyla says. "Both of you." She looks at me. "I underestimated you."

"Ditto," I say.

Twyla rushes down the stairs, blocking my view of Summer.

"Are you OK, Mum?" Hannah steps out from behind me.

"I'm fine," I say, checking her for marks and injuries. "How about you?"

I grab her and squeeze tight.

"You're trembling," I say. "You need to sit down and drink water."

"I don't know why I'm shaking," Hannah says watching her shuddering hands. "I'm not scared." She looks at me. "At first, I was scared, but now I'm hyped. It's a rush. I feel like I can do anything."

"It's adrenalin." I guide her toward the stairs to the third floor. "It'll stop in a couple of hours," I say from experience.

"We were awesome!" Hannah brags as we climb the stairs side-by-side. "I wish we had recorded it. We were like superheroes. Who knew we could fight like that?" she huffs, amazed. "We disarmed a murderer!" Her chest heaves and her breaths are fast. "I feel unstoppable, like I'm capable of anything!"

"Me too," I agree, horrified of what I might be capable of.

"We kicked butt." Hannah lets out a half chuckle.

"You get that from me."

CHAPTER 33

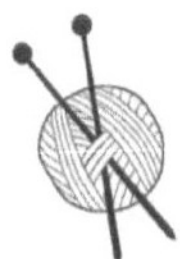

Saturday, June 4th

I lock my phone screen and shove the phone in my back pocket, then comb my fingers through my curls with a long, heavy sigh. I sink into the booth at the pub, processing Eric's text.

"What is it, my dear?" Connie asks, handing me a bouquet of balloons. "Bad news?"

The text was neither good nor bad. The information he gave me was neither good nor bad.

"No," I reply, tying the police-car shaped mylar balloon to the back of the guest-of-honour's chair. "I asked Eric to find out if there were bullets in the gun. He just texted me the answer."

"The gun that Summer pointed at Hannah?" Connie asks, horrified by the mere mention of the event. "What good comes from knowing, my dear? It's time to stop tormenting yourself and move on. Summer was arrested, and you and Hannah weren't injured. In fact, the experience empowered Hannah. She has a newfound, mature confidence that she didn't have before."

"I'd still rather she never had the experience, but there's no point in wishing the past was different."

"Was it loaded?" April asks, placing a square glass vase at the centre of the table.

"No," I say, tying a gold balloon to the chair. "Twyla was right. It wasn't loaded."

"This doesn't invalidate the fear you felt," Connie reminds me, dropping golf balls and fishing lures—hooks removed—into the glass vase. "As far as you and Hannah knew, the gun was loaded. You were at the mercy of a murderer." She pokes a blue daisy into the jar, then a yellow daisy.

"I still don't understand why Twyla took the ammunition but left Summer's gun behind," April says.

"Apparently, she was authorized to have it," I reply, recalling Twyla's explanation, but most of it is a blur because I was still in shock when she explained it to me. "It's complicated, but it had something to do with the original threat to her life. Anyway, because everyone believed Summer was dead, and the gun was part of her belongings, and not part of the murder investigation, Twyla didn't have the authority to seize the weapon. However, she had the authority to seize the ammunition."

"Thank goodness she did," Connie comments.

"She saved a life," I say.

April and Connie will assume I'm referring to

Hannah's life, but I'm recalling my urge to end Summer's life with her own gun.

"What else is bothering you, Megnificent?" April asks, poking more yellow and blue daisies into the centrepiece.

"Am I a bad person?" I ask, untangling the balloon ribbons and separating a gold balloon from the bouquet.

"Bad people don't wonder if they're bad people," April replies. She sets a hat, sash, and giant pin-on badge at the guest of honour's seat. The badge reads, *I'm retired, not expired,* and features a border of flashing blue lights. "Also, I only hang out with good people, and you're my best friend, making you, by definition, a good person."

"You didn't kill her, my dear. You didn't even pick up the gun."

"But I wanted to," I admit. "And I was mid-lunge when Twyla stopped me."

Connie lays down the party accessories and hugs me.

"You aren't a bad person, and you mustn't pay attention to the inane ramblings of an unstable mind." She pulls away and starts assembling the next centre-piece. "Summer's speech about good and bad people was to justify her own actions. It was nonsense. Don't let her get in your head."

"Connie's right," April says. She grins. "Any parent would have the same urge. Heck, lots of parents would have reached for the gun without a second thought. You aren't a bad person, Megadoodle, you're a mother. It's how we're wired."

"Megan!"

Just as I place the familiar voice, its owner appears in front of me.

"Maria? Why are you in Harmony Lake?"

"I have something for you."

Maria pulls two envelopes from her bag and hands one to me and one to April.

"Thanks," I say.

"What is it?" April asks.

"Gift certificates for a weekend at SoulSpring Spa and Retreat," Maria replies. "Before I resign, I want to compensate you for the inconveniences during your last visit."

"You already refunded us for our stay," April reminds her.

"The refund didn't seem adequate to compensate for everything that happened."

"Thank you," I say, doubting I'll use my gift certificate because the last place I want to visit is the scene of Summer's crimes.

April and Connie also thank Maria, with as much as enthusiasm as one can muster when they're given a gift that they know they won't use.

"Wait a few weeks before you use them," Maria warns. "Nadira is away and a guest chef is filling in for her." She uses her hands like a verbal eraser. "The guest chef is great, but most people want Nadira's food."

"Did Nadira go somewhere exciting?" Connie asks.

"Northern Ireland," Maria replies. "She won another World Luxury Spa and Restaurant Award. She's attending the gala award ceremony in Belfast."

"Good for her!" April chimes in.

"Every guest who was at the spa that weekend will get gift certificates before I leave," Maria announces. "I won't be able to hand-deliver them, but I wanted to deliver yours and Billie's."

"You saw Billie?" I ask. "How is she?"

"I see Billie all the time," Maria says. "We've spent a lot of time together since…" Maria shakes her head and refocuses. "She's doing much better than last time you saw her," Maria replies. "Her morning sickness is better than it was." She taps her cell phone then hands it to me. "This is her first ultrasound."

"Awww," Connie, April, and I swoon over the grainy image.

"It was nice of you to visit her," Connie comments. "Billie lost her two best friends in three days."

"Billie is amazing," Maria says. "She has such a great attitude, despite everything that happened. And we have so much in common. We grew up in the same town and know the same people, and Summer changed our lives. We've become close since Mother's Day. Billie promises to visit Harmony Lake and bring the baby to meet everyone."

"When is her baby due?" I ask.

"December," Maria replies. "After Summer's sentencing hearing."

I nod.

Summer's confession makes it difficult for her to plead not guilty to killing her sister. In exchange for a guilty plea, the prosecution agreed to give her a say in which penitentiary she'll serve her sentence and accommodate her request for certain creature comforts that are scarce in prison.

"At least she's sparing us the stress of a trial," Connie says, looking for a silver lining.

"You drove all the way to Harmony Lake to deliver gift certificates?" I ask.

"Twyla is signing her offer today, and I tagged along so we could look at houses," she replies. "I went to Knitorious first. The lady said I'd find you at the pub."

"Congratulations to Twyla," Connie says. "We're proud to have her join the ranks of Harmony Lake's finest."

"Thank you," Maria says. "I'll tell her." She looks at me. "Thanks again, Megan, for putting in a kind word with Eric."

"I didn't," I say. "He inquired about her when I told him about Summer's murder. Everyone gave her glowing reviews. I mentioned she might be looking for a new opportunity. Twyla did the rest. She impressed him during the interview. If we're thanking each other, thank you again for alerting Twyla that Hannah and I were in the stairwell with Summer. You might have saved my daughter's life."

Maria witnessed Hannah and I arguing in the lobby when I tried to drag Hannah to our room. She also noticed the person she believed was Autumn sneak past us into the stairwell. Maria admitted it hadn't occurred to her that she sneaked into the stairwell to intercept us. She worried that something had upset her and caused her to rush out of the lobby. And she worried about Hannah and I because she had seen us arguing. She used her two-way radio to contact the attendant stationed on the third floor and asked her to check on Autumn and to check on us. The attendant contacted her when none of us were in our rooms. Maria then asked the second-floor attendant if we had emerged on the second floor and became worried when she learned we hadn't.

Twyla had just returned from rescuing the injured hiker. Maria told her that Autumn—who she didn't yet know was Summer—Hannah, and I went into the stairwell and never came out. Twyla cordoned off the stairs, took the elevator to the third floor, and snuck into the stairwell to search for us. She heard voices and realized something was wrong on the second-floor landing.

Twyla knew Summer's gun was not loaded, but knew Hannah and I believed it was. She tried to lure Summer upstairs so Hannah and I could get away. It didn't work, but she provoked Summer to point the gun away from Hannah, giving us the chance we needed to escape.

Twyla later told me that she considered ambushing Summer but worried that Hannah or I would end up badly injured, or worse, if we toppled down the cement stairs.

"Her predecessor's retirement party starts in a

couple of hours." April flicks the police-car shaped mylar balloon. "We're just setting up."

"I see that," Maria says, adjusting a centrepiece so it is precisely in the centre of the table. "May I help?"

"You don't need to help," I say. "Thank you, though."

"No, I want to help," Maria insists. "I'll be a Harmony Lake resident soon, and I plan to immerse myself in the community."

"In that case"—I hand her a roll of crime scene tape—"this is for the guest of honour's table."

"Have you found somewhere to live?" April asks.

"I don't want to jinx it," Maria says, crossing her fingers. "But we loved one house we viewed today. As soon as Twyla finishes signing paperwork at the police station, we're meeting with our agent to make an offer."

"Good luck!" Connie says.

"Thanks," Maria says, wrapping the table with yellow tape. "Everything is coming together. It's like the universe wants us to move here. I have a second interview next week at a local spa. I have a good feeling about it. I'm pretty sure they're going to offer me the manager job."

"Which spa?" Connie asks, lowering her reading glasses to her eyes.

Before Maria finishes telling Connie which of Harmony Lake's two spas might hire her, Connie is tapping her phone screen.

"Who are you texting?" I ask.

"Everyone, my dear." Connie sends her text and

looks at Maria. "We'll flood the spa with recommendations to hire you." She winks.

"People are so nice here," Maria comments, wrapping the back of the guest-of-honour's chair with crime scene tape. "Everyone is welcoming and friendly. Harmony Lake is nothing like the small town where Twyla and I grew up. In our town, everyone knew everyone else's business, and the town's collective pastime was gossip. I'm glad Harmony Lake isn't like that."

Connie, April, and I look at each other, eyes wide with raised eyebrows.

"Who wants to tell her?" April asks.

"Not me!" I blurt, beating Connie.

"Me neither." Connie flicks her wrist and continues assembling centrepieces with her back to us.

"Tell me what?" Maria asks.

"Nothing," we say, smiling.

CLICK HERE to read an exclusive Bait & Stitch bonus scene!

ALSO BY REAGAN DAVIS

Knit One Murder Two

Killer Cables

Murder & Merino

Twisted Stitches

Son of a Stitch

Crime Skein

Rest In Fleece

Life Crafter Death

In Stitchness and in Health

Bait & Stitch

Murder It Seams

Neigbourhood Swatch: A Knitorious Cozy Mystery Short Story

Click here to sign up for Reagan Davis' email list to be notified of new releases and special offers.

Follow Reagan Davis on Amazon

Follow Reagan Davis on Facebook, Bookbub, Goodreads, and Instagram

ABOUT THE AUTHOR

Reagan Davis doesn't really exist. She is a pen name for the real author who lives in the suburbs of Toronto with her husband, two kids, and a menagerie of pets. When she's not planning the perfect murder, she enjoys knitting, reading, eating too much chocolate, and drinking too much Diet Coke. The author is an established knitwear designer who regularly publishes individual patterns and is a contributor to many knitting books and magazines. I'd tell you her real name, but then I'd have to kill you. (Just kidding! Sort of.)

http://www.ReaganDavis.com/email